Before Darby could open the door of her car, Cody had opened it for her. Lifting her up in his arms, he carried her through the snow to her house. . . .

They were both laughing when he finally set her down, groaning about his aching back. She unlocked the door, then turned to say good night.

"You still object to me kissing you?" Cody asked softly.

Darby nodded, but when his lips brushed hers, she didn't pull away. She tasted cold and sweet to him, and he tasted warm and male to her. She couldn't ever remember wanting this much or needing like this.

"Cody, please," she murmured.

"I'm not going to kiss you or touch you in any way—not until you want it as much as I do."

His mouth was so close, so agonizingly close now. Their breath was one in the cold night air as he moved against her, assaulting her senses.

"Cody, please—"

"Please what?"

She sighed; she could fight it no longer. "Please kiss me. . . ."

WHAT ARE *LOVESWEPT* ROMANCES?

They are stories of true romance and touching emotion. We believe those two very important ingredients are constants in our highly sensual and very believable stories in the *LOVESWEPT* line. Our goal is to give you, the reader, stories of consistently high quality that may sometimes make you laugh, sometimes make you cry, but are always fresh and creative and contain many delightful surprises within their pages.

Most romance fans read an enormous number of books. Those they truly love, they keep. Others may be traded with friends and soon forgotten. We hope that each *LOVESWEPT* romance will be a treasure—a "keeper." We will always try to publish

LOVE STORIES YOU'LL NEVER FORGET
BY AUTHORS YOU'LL ALWAYS REMEMBER

The Editors

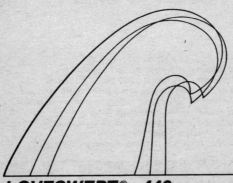

LOVESWEPT® • 440

Lori Copeland
'Tiz The Season

 BANTAM BOOKS
NEW YORK • TORONTO • LONDON • SYDNEY • AUCKLAND

'TIZ THE SEASON

A Bantam Book / December 1990

LOVESWEPT® and the wave device are registered
trademarks of Bantam Books, a division of
Bantam Doubleday Dell Publishing Group, Inc.
Registered in U.S. Patent
and Trademark Office and elsewhere.

If you would be interested in receiving protective vinyl
covers for your Loveswept books, please write to this
address for information:

Loveswept
Bantam Books
P. O. Box 985
Hicksville, NY 11802

ISBN 0-553-44071-3

Published simultaneously in the United States and Canada

Bantam Books are published by Bantam Books, a division
of Bantam Doubleday Dell Publishing Group, Inc. Its trademark, consisting of the words "Bantam Books" and the
portrayal of a rooster, is Registered in U.S. Patent and
Trademark Office and in other countries. Marca Regis-
trada. Bantam Books, 666 Fifth Avenue, New York, New
York 10103.

PRINTED IN THE UNITED STATES OF AMERICA

OPM   0 9 8 7 6 5 4 3 2 1

One

"Good morning, Boston! Temperatures should be in the high thirties with a threat of snow moving in by evening. Only twenty-three shopping days left until Christmas—"

Darby switched on her hair drier and drowned out the announcer's voice. "Tiz the season to be jolly," she grumbled as she tossed her wet hair over her head, then bent forward to dry it.

Darby was not in the holiday spirit. The work load at the office had been so heavy this fall, she'd barely had time to grab meals. Christmas shopping was not a priority.

When she switched the drier off five minutes later, the radio was playing soft music, which was overwhelmed by the bustling activity in the street outside.

The construction had started again. During the past few weeks the rumble of blasting and the whine of heavy machinery jostling up and down the street had become a normal part of her daily routine. The three-million-dollar project to install new sewer lines in the Boston suburbs had just made it to her neighborhood.

For five years Darby had scraped and saved for a down payment on the condo in Gildersleeve Addition, a small, affluent residential community located thirty minutes outside Boston. And what had she gained by moving out of the noisy, congested city?

Heavy machinery and more traffic tie-ups.

The dirt, noise, and confusion were a constant source of annoyance, and Darby longed to see the project completed.

She glanced at her watch again and was alarmed to see that the second hand had already crept to five past eight. She was running behind.

Stepping inside her closet, she slipped on her shoes, glancing at the mirror for one final inspection.

Today was very important. She was trying a critical case. If she won, her victory would practically assure that she would become a full partner in the prestigious legal firm of Yates, Bates, Slag & Choleric. She'd dedicated eighteen hours a day to the firm for the past three years, and Darby felt she had earned the compensation.

Glancing at her watch again, she picked up her briefcase and purse and let herself out the front door. Outside, the sound of the bulldozer was deafening. She gritted her teeth as she eyed the dozer sourly. "I should have known," she muttered. The large, growling machine was blocking her driveway.

It was the second time this week she had been forced to ask the operator to move his heavy equipment so that she could back out of her drive.

Striding to her corporate-gray BMW, she tossed her briefcase and purse into the backseat. Then she picked her way carefully down the drive. A heavy rain the night before had turned the already saturated ground into a muddy marsh.

She stepped gingerly through the shallow pools of standing water, avoiding the softer areas, praying that she wouldn't ruin her new shoes. She'd splurged on the navy-blue Italian pumps, and she didn't relish the thought of seeing them covered with black muck.

Incredibly the noise was even louder as she approached the massive earthmover. Cupping her hands to her mouth, she shouted, "Hey!"

The huge machine's long, clawlike arm was dipping into the ground, its jagged teeth biting into chunks of earth, then depositing them on the side of the drive.

"Hey!" she shouted again, realizing that it wasn't going to be easy to divert the operator's attention. He seemed to be thoroughly absorbed in his work.

But Darby was determined. This morning she would face Judge "Give 'em Hell" Moorhouse and he was famous as a stickler for punctuality. Darby knew that if she wasn't walking into his courtroom in exactly forty-five minutes, she could expect trouble. Big trouble. Judge Moorhouse had no qualms about dressing down a tardy attorney in front of a jury and a packed gallery. In fact, he seemed to take delight in watching a young lawyer squirm in agony.

Darby shouted again. The memory of a thunderous glare on Judge Moorhouse's face lent a note of urgency to her voice now. "Hey! I need to get out of my drive!" She was practically screaming.

The man finally glanced up, frowning.

"You're going to have to move this thing!" she shouted above the roar of the machine.

The man shook his head, still frowning. Darby could see that he couldn't make out what she was saying.

"My car!" Darby pointed to the BMW. "You have to move. I need to get out!"

She noticed that this morning a different man was operating the dozer. Yesterday a skinny teenager had been behind the wheel. The man behind the wheel this morning appeared to be older, more seasoned.

Leaving the machine running, the operator kicked open the door and stuck his head out. "You want something?"

No, I'm just standing in mud up to my patoosie, shrieking like a banshee, to amuse myself, Darby thought in frustration.

"You're blocking the drive. You'll have to move so I can get out."

The operator motioned for her to wait a minute, and then he calmly climbed down from the cab. As he removed his hard hat, his eyes ran over her with lazy proficiency, lightly skimming her navy-blue suit and crisp white blouse.

Darby felt her pulse quicken under his perusal, something that rarely happened in a man's presence. She stiffened her spine and frowned, unwilling to admit that this man could easily induce such a reaction.

He was tall, dark, and undeniably handsome. He had curly, light-brown hair that hugged the nape of his neck, and his skin was tanned golden brown. His wavy hair gave him a deceptively youthful appearance, although the rugged creases around his eyes and forehead told Darby that he was probably in his late thirties.

He also had incredibly direct, liquid blue eyes.

And those eyes were focused entirely on her now.

"Something I can do for you, ma'am?"

Darby was rarely tongue-tied, but when her eyes lifted to meet his, the sudden electrical contact had the strangest effect on her. She suddenly felt weak in the knees, and sixteen years old again.

"I . . . I need to get out of my drive. How long will you be digging this . . ." She gestured to the hole in the ground helplessly.

The operator turned his gaze to follow the crimson tip of her manicured nail. "Trench?"

"Hole," she conceded. "You'll have to move your machine. I can't get out."

The man's gaze shifted back to her, his eyes smoothly skimming again over her business suit and expensive pumps. Darby felt her cheeks growing warm as his gaze moved over in no apparent hurry to leave.

Nice, the man decided. She was a little too haughty for his taste, but a definite looker. "Sorry for the incovenience, ma'am. Give me ten minutes, and I'll be out of your way."

Darby's dark eyes returned impatiently to her watch. "I don't have ten minutes. I'm late as it is."

"Then I'll try to make it five."

Darby frowned at the growling machine. There had to be a way to end the impasse. "Do you have a permit to dig this ditch?" Her tone was cold as she hoped to intimidate him. The ploy had worked beautifully on the other operator.

"Yes, ma'am."

Darby's brows raised. "And I suppose you're a demolition *expert*?"

His left brow lifted ever so slightly. "Do I need to be?"

"I've heard blasting. Surely your company has the proper permits to blast?"

Their eyes met and locked.

"I'm sure they do," he returned calmly.

She could see from the rigid set of his jaw that he intended to hang tough, but that was his mistake. Darby Piper could hang tougher.

Both sets of eyes remained stubbornly fixed, both brimming with spunk now.

"And you?" She quirked an impervious brow. "Do *you* have a valid license to drive that dozer?" Her threat was so thinly veiled that it even made her blush. But darn it! He was going to be responsible for her tardiness, and her dressing down!

"Yes, ma'am, I sure do." He glanced toward her car. "And I suppose you have a valid license to drive the BMW?"

Darby's jaw firmed. They were getting nowhere. The man clearly had no intention of cooperating with her. "Look, I don't have time to argue. Just move the dozer."

"Give me ten minutes, and I'll be out of your

way," he repeated, and Darby detected just a hint of rebellion in his attitude now.

She supposed that a man with his enthralling good looks was accustomed to charming women. But she was in no mood to be charmed.

Drawing a deep breath, she sent him her most patronizing look. "Ten minutes. Not a moment longer."

"Fifteen minutes—only I'd suggest you remain inside the house until I tell you it's okay to leave."

Darby fumed. But she knew if she argued any more the fifteen would become twenty. Turning, Darby started to make her way back to the house, daintily sidestepping the mudholes again.

The operator watched her go, a smile twitching at the corners of his mouth.

Exactly fifteen minutes later, he watched her march out her front door and once again carefully pick her way down the driveway.

The ditch was finished. But now a huge mound of dirt was heaped beside the edge of her drive.

It was clear to Darby that the man had deliberately piled the dirt there so that she would just barely have enough room to squeeze her BMW around it.

When she glanced back at the dozer, she saw the operator sitting in the cab, drinking a cup of coffee, his feet arrogantly cocked on the dash.

Shooting him a murderous look, Darby got into

her car, adjusted her rearview mirror, fastened her seat belt, and started the engine.

She shifted into reverse and began to back the car out of the drive, edging past the mound of fresh dirt, going quickly to show the man what a proficient driver she was. Just as she was growing smug knowing he had not bested her, she heard a funny whine.

A moment later she grimaced as she heard the wheels of the BMW spinning.

She glanced into her rearview mirror and saw the dozer operator grinning over the rim of his coffee cup.

Grinning!

At her!

Taking a deep breath, she pressed the accelerator harder.

The wheels spun in the loose dirt but refused to budge.

Pressing the accelerator more firmly, Darby moved the gear shift from reverse into first and began rocking the car gently back and forth. Although the car lurched to the right and then to the left, the wheels still had no traction.

Losing her patience, Darby jammed the gearshift into reverse and floored the accelerator. The motor roared.

The back wheels spun like a top, sending a plume of blue smoke spiraling into the air.

Glancing into the rearview mirror, she saw the

dozer operator yawn, then nonchalantly lean forward to fill his coffee cup from a thermos.

Gunning the motor again, Darby felt the back wheels spinning. Dirt and rocks flew as she made one last frantic, frenzied bid for freedom.

Whoommmm!

She realized that she was making a complete fool of herself. Her efforts were only embedding the car deeper into the mire.

Clamping her eyes shut in frustration, she drew another long, cleansing breath. Why was this happening to *her*? She was making an idiot of herself in front of that smirking worker.

The man had leaned back and made himself comfortable as he watched the back wheels of the BMW dig deeper and deeper into the bog. The car was up to its hubs in the nasty slime.

With a defeated sigh Darby faced the obvious. She was stuck. Hopelessly stuck.

And it was all that man's fault.

She jerked open her car door and stepped out, wincing and gritting her teeth as her foot sank deeply into the slime. Murmuring an obscenity, she looked down to see the mud oozing over the rim of her new pump.

Jerking her foot out of her shoe, she limped to the garage and yanked up the door.

Hefting a grocery sack full of newspapers, she marched back outside. Maybe if placing newspapers beneath the wheels worked on ice, it might work on mud. Her hose were completely ruined now, and she didn't even want to think about her shoes. She removed the remaining pump and shoved it into the bag as she started back to the car.

Tramping through the mudholes now, she was determined to salvage what was left of her pride.

The *jerk* was still in the dozer, calmly drinking his coffee and thumbing through the sports section of the newspaper.

She squatted down and carefully arranged the newspapers beneath both wheels.

A moment later she slid behind the wheel, and the motor sprang into action again.

For one brief, gratifying instant Darby thought that her tactic might be working. But a moment later the tires angrily belched the newspapers out into the ditch.

Really angry now, Darby stomped hard on the accelerator, determined to manhandle the car if necessary. The tires roared in protest.

Only when her windshield was covered with a blinding layer of mud did she admit defeat.

She slammed out of the car and marched over to the dozer to rap briskly on the window.

The man casually set aside his cup and rolled down the window.

"Yes, ma'am?"

"I'm stuck."

Amusement flickered in his eyes. "Yes, ma'am."

"Well, what do you plan to do about it?"

He appeared surprised. "I wasn't aware that it was my place to do anything about it."

"You *deliberately* put that dirt where I couldn't get around it," she accused.

Their eyes locked.

"You were supposed to wait until I told you that you could leave," he reminded her.

"*I* waited fifteen minutes."

"Ah, but *I* didn't say that you could leave yet," he said simply.

"Now listen to me. This is all your fault. You can just help me get my car out of that mudhole!" She glanced anxiously at her watch again, then groaned. It was eight-thirty!

"I don't think so."

Darby's head snapped up. "You *will* get my car out of that mud," she repeated ominously.

"Or what?"

"Or else!'

"Now, ma'am!"—he touched the brim of his hard hat respectfully—"I'd really like to help you, but you see, I just can't."

"Oh, really?" Darby met his gaze antagonistically. "And exactly why *can't* you help me?"

He smiled, lowering his head subserviently. "*I* don't have a license to tow."

Darby glared at him, fighting the urge to scream. He was the most irritating, overbearing fool she had ever encountered.

"Your name?" she demanded, fumbling blindly in her bag for a pen and paper. She was going to report him; there was no longer any doubt about it.

The man started the dozer engine and then motioned contritely that he couldn't understand a word she was saying.

Drawing back, Darby couldn't believe his audacity. As the man continued to pump the gas feed, the dozer's roar became deafening.

How dare he, she seethed. How dare he treat her this way!

Furiously, she whirled and strode back toward her house. She had no choice: She had to call the court clerk to request a delay, using the pitiful excuse that she was a prisoner in her own driveway.

Two

"Ordinarily, I would let the incident pass," Darby said into the receiver." But the man's attitude was inexcusable." She leaned closer to the public phone, trying to block out the noise in the busy courthouse. She'd arrived by taxi at ten o'clock, still fuming over the run-in with the dozer operator. She was not going to let the incident this morning pass without comment.

"I can't imagine one of my employees acting in such a manner," the owner of C.B. Construction soothed. "Let me say on behalf of the firm—er—what was your name again, ma'am?"

"Darby Piper."

"On behalf of the firm, Ms. Piper, please accept my sincere apologies," the man said.

"I will expect the employee to be reprimanded."

"Oh, yes, ma'am. I'll have one of my men speak to him immediately—you say you didn't get his name?"

"No." Darby knew she should have, but he had been throttling his blasted dozer so loud! "But he was operating a bulldozer in front of my house this morning. He shouldn't be too hard to locate." Anyone as cocky as that man would surely stand out in a crowd, she reasoned.

"Well, of course there are several men working on dozers out there, but—what was your address, Ms. . . ." The man appeared to search for her name again.

"Ms. Piper."

"Yes . . . Ms. Piper. And your address?"

"Seven nine three six four Sugarlane."

"Seven nine three six four Sugarlane?"

"Yes. Please let him know that I didn't appreciate his attitude, or that he made me late for work."

"Oh, yes, ma'am, and please assure your husband—"

"I'm not married."

"Oh?" There was a small pause.

"You will take care of the matter promptly?"

"Yes, ma"am."

"Thank you."

"You're most welcome—Ms. . . . ?"

"Piper."

"Yes, Ms. Piper. You can count on me."

Replacing the receiver, Darby grinned triumphantly.

Ha! Let that overbearing idiot put that in his conceited little pipe and smoke it!

By the time Darby reached her office, it was close to two.

Gail, the redheaded receptionist, grinned as she handed Darby a stack of messages. "Judge Moorhouse's clerk called."

Darby's heart sank. "What did she say?"

"I quote: 'His Honor is not amused by Ms. Piper's excuse for her delay. He requests Ms. Piper's presence in chambers before court convenes tomorrow morning.' "

"Great. Just great," Darby muttered.

"You really were stuck in your own driveway?"

"Yes, I was stuck in my own driveway. Trapped by an overbearing construction worker." Darby managed a weak smile. "Is Carter in?"

"He is. Shall I ring him?"

"Don't bother," she said, absently sorting through the messages. "I'll just go on in."

Carter Bates was a senior member of the firm and Darby's mentor. She often discussed cases with Carter, using him as a sounding board. She knew that she could be certain of his vote when the nomination to accept her as a full partner was presented. The fact that he was a lovable old bear of a man didn't hurt, either. That made him seem more like a favorite uncle than a colleague.

"How'd the Howard case turn out this morning?" Gail asked.

Darby grinned. "I won."

Darby knocked on Carter's door a moment later. Entering at his invitation, she braced herself for a teasing.

"Well, if it isn't Ms. Piper." Carter flashed her a grin. "Is it dark outside yet?"

Darby flushed, then smiled back. "I am a little late."

"I hear you had a bit of trouble this morning."

"A bit," Darby acknowledged as she settled on a chair in front of his desk.

Carter's office was decorated exactly as she wanted her office to be someday. The walls were covered with rich walnut paneling that gleamed with the patina of mellow age. Heavy drapes in federal blue hung at the window to mask the late-afternoon sun that would soon slant across the massive walnut desk. She adored the room's understated elegance.

Carter's chair squeaked comfortably as he redistributed his bulky frame. "Yes, I hear Bill Moorhouse isn't too happy with you."

"To say the least. I've been invited for a private audience in his chambers tomorrow morning."

She shrugged. "Maybe he wants to offer to pay my towing charge."

Carter chuckled. "Think so?"

She grinned. "Not likely."

"I wouldn't worry about it." Carter laid his pencil on the desk, leaned back, and folded his hands over his protruding stomach. "I heard you won the Howard case. Congratulations."

"Thanks, I earned it." She winked at him playfully.

"So, what else is on your mind this morning?"

Darby smiled, relaxing for the first time that day. "I know I don't need an excuse to visit with you . . . but I have a case I'd like your opinion on."

"You've got it." Carter smiled. "What's the problem?"

"It concerns a joint litigation. A neighborhood has filed an injunction against one of its neighbors, Cordell Benderman. They want Mr. Benderman to remove the elaborate Christmas decorations he displays in his yard each year. They claim the traffic the spectacle draws is becoming a public nuisance. The plaintiffs can't get in or out of their street because so many sightseers drive by to see his display."

"Do we have a bunch of Scrooges here?" Carter asked.

"No, the plaintiffs have a legitimate gripe. Not only are they forced to contend with heavy vehicular traffic, but the man's Christmas lights are connected to a timer, and apparently they stay on half the night. It seems that Mr. Benderman could sleep through a nuclear holocaust, so the blinding light and racket he causes don't bother him in the least."

"What's this Benderman got in his display?"

"Everything but the Ghost of Christmas Past. His yard is extremely—shall we say, roomy? There's a nativity scene, complete with a stable and *real* animals. *Every* tree and bush in his yard is strung with multicolored lights, twinkling over a fairyland of Santa's toyshop. In his side yard he has shepherds and sheep lit in pale blue and angels suspended in midair, blowing trumpets— complete with periodic trumpeted blasts of "Hark the Herald Angels Sing."

Carter shook his head, chuckling.

"This display goes up right after Thanksgiving and remains until New Year's Day. Cars are lined up for blocks, and . . . oh. Mr. Benderman pipes Christmas carols outside too."

"Sounds like quite a charming display," Carter said.

"Charming, but the neighbors are threatening to deck Mr. Benderman's halls with ball bats."

"So? How do you intend to handle it?"

"Well, first I plan to go by there tonight and see the display firsthand. I'm meeting with the litigants later tomorrow." Darby winced. "That is if there's anything left of me after Judge Moorhouse is finished."

"I'm sure everything will be fine," Carter assured her. "You're a capable young attorney, and Bill Moorhouse knows it."

"Thanks, Carter. I really needed that. After the day I've had, I was beginning to feel like a complete incompetent. Getting my car stuck, of all things, and in my own yard."

Darby was surprised to discover that she could almost laugh about the incident now. But that moron on the dozer owed her a new pair of shoes. "Of course, if that *man* hadn't piled dirt in my way, I wouldn't have gotten stuck."

"That *man?*" Carter laughed.

"Carter, it wasn't amusing. There are gentlemen, and there are men. This one was a *man*. I have never been so angry in my entire life."

"Well, you have to admit it must have been an amusing sight. Darby Piper, a woman who rarely has a hair out of place, wading through mud up to her ankles, spitting like a tomcat."

"I don't see anything amusing about it," Darby countered, "and I'll never forgive that man for the trouble he caused me. I've already called his boss."

"Ah the life and times of Darby Piper." Carter had that twinkle in his eyes that always managed to soothe Darby's bruised ego. "If I were you, I wouldn't let him get to me."

"Ha!" That *man* would be the last person on earth to get to her.

Darby stood up and leaned over to give Carter a warm hug. "Thanks. You always make me feel better."

"That's why I'm here. Otherwise, I'd have retired years ago. . . . By the way, what's that Benderman's address? Vivian and I are baby-sitting the grandchildren tonight, and I'd like to drive them by to see—"

"Carter!"

Carter was still chuckling when Darby left his office a moment later.

As she entered her own office she was struck again by how cold her office was compared to Carter's. There were two navy-upholstered chairs, but the rest of the office was conventional glass and chrome.

Darby sat behind the steel desk and began going over her notes on the case that would go to the jury at the end of the week.

At six that evening as she slipped the last of her folders into her leather case, Vance Choleric, one of the firm's senior partners, stuck his head through the doorway. "Care to stop by Puddigan's and have a drink with me?"

"Sounds great." Darby snapped her briefcase shut, pleased that he'd thought to ask her. There was nothing personal between Vance and her, but

Darby always welcomed the opportunity to socialize with the firm's senior partners.

"Want me to drive?" Darby offered as they took
the elevator down together. The garage had
dropped off her car at four that afternoon.

"Do you mind? Mine's still in the garage."

"What's wrong this time?"

"Who knows? Every week the mechanic finds
some problem that costs a hundred and twenty-
five dollars to fix. It's uncanny. I can practically
depend on it. One hundred twenty-five dollars.
Right on the button."

They chatted amicably as Darby drove to Puddigan's, a colorful "watering hole" frequented by
Boston's professional crowd. Taking Darby's arm,
Vance threaded their way across the crowded
room. She was forced to sidestep quickly twice to
avoid bumping into harried waitresses balancing
trays loaded with drinks.

Vance quickly claimed an empty table. A moment
later Darby slid into a chair opposite him, heaving a sigh.

"Long day?" Vance asked, signaling a waitress.

"Very," Darby returned. "I'm exhausted, and I
still have to stop at the market before I go home."

Vance ordered a vodka on the rocks and a white
wine. Turning back to Darby, he grinned. "I
heard you drew the Santa Claus Caper."

Darby frowned. "Santa Claus Caper? Where did
that come from?"

"Pete." Pete was a law clerk in the firm whose wit was legendary. "He told me to tell you he'll be happy to do your research, though he wants me to warn you that he'll be biased in the defendant's favor."

"Biased?"

"Yeah. He doesn't want Santa to cross his name off his list." Vance winked. "I hear the old man checks it twice."

Darby massaged her temples. It was amazing she only had a headache. Lord, the Santa Claus Caper. She'd never live this one down.

The waitress returned with their drinks. After tasting his vodka, Vance turned his attention to Darby. "I'm glad we have these few moments alone, Darby. I've been wanting to talk to you."

His tone caught Darby's interest as she lifted her glass of white wine. "Anything wrong?"

"Not at all. In fact, everything is right. As you know, I was skeptical when Carter hired you. Being a born 'male chauvinist pig' "—he grinned—"I couldn't believe that a woman as pretty as you could have your zeal and dedication to the law, much less your remarkable talent for the business."

Darby returned his smile warmly. She had been aware of Vance's reservations; he'd certainly made no attempt to hide his doubts. Apparently her efforts to win him over had worked.

Vance leaned forward, resting his elbows on the

table. His eyes met hers solemnly. "I'm proud of you, Darby. You're one of the finest young attorneys I've ever had the privilege to work with. I want you to know that, in my opinion, you deserve the firm's next full partnership."

Darby's heart grew warm with pleasure. Vance couldn't have given her a nicer Christmas present. Everything she'd hoped for, dreamed of, was about to come true. A full partnership . . . and before she was thirty-five.

Lifting her glass, she offered him a silent tribute. "Thank you, Vance. I appreciate your vote of confidence."

"I propose a toast." He lifted his glass. "To a new 'almost partner.' "

Darby smiled as they touched glasses; the tiny *ping* was almost lost in the cacophony of sound around them.

Raising the glass to her lips, Darby's hand suddenly froze.

Just two tables away sat that stubborn dozer operator with two of his red-necked cronies, and he was staring straight at her.

Horrified, she watched as he calmly smiled, lifting his glass in a mocking salute.

Refusing to acknowledge him, she quickly averted her gaze. The *jerk,* she fumed. Who did he think he was? Vance had referred to himself as a chauvinist, but he was Prince Charming compared to that crude, overbearing dirt-digger!

The man lowered his glass, unperturbed by her cold reception.

Cordell Benderman's glance slid back to the man Ms. Darby Piper was sitting with. He looked like a big shot wearing an expensive suit. He also looked too old for her. It figured.

He took a sip of his beer, wondered who the guy was, then wondered why he was wondering. If she wanted to date a man old enough to be her father, it was no sweat off his brow.

He looked back at Darby to find her looking at him.

He winked.

Darby's head snapped back, but not before she saw the smile quirking the corners of his mouth.

The man returned his attention to the conversation his two friends were having. *That little snip was treating him like he was something nasty left in her yard by the neighbor's dog.*

Darby carefully refrained from looking at the man's table. It was another twenty long minutes later before she felt she could make a polite getaway.

Drinking the last of her wine, she smiled and reached for her purse. "Well, it's getting late."

Vance stood and motioned for the check. As they walked past the construction worker's table, Darby pointedly looked the other way. The man was undoubtedly swilling beer and rating the "chicks" in the bar on a scale of one to ten, Darby guessed as she wove her way through the crowd. She didn't look back as she strode out the front door.

A wind had sprung up, and there was a threat of snow in the air. "Just what I need," Darby complained as she huddled deeper into the lining of her leather coat, "*snow* on top of all the mud in front of my house."

Vance laughed. "It's not going to snow. The weatherman thinks now that the front will miss us."

"I sincerely hope he's right."

As Darby dropped Vance off in front of his town house, the first flakes of snow had begun to fall.

"You going straight home?" Vance turned up his collar, glancing sourly at the ash-colored sky. "It looks like our illustrious forecasters have missed it again."

"I have to run by the market, then I think I'll swing through a neighborhood to check out a Christmas display."

"A Christmas display?"

"Sure!" Darby grinned as she waved good-bye. "Tiz the season, you know."

At a little before eight the BMW's headlights caught the arched entry to Cordell Benderman's subdivision.

Darby signaled a turn while her wipers tried hard to keep up with the thick flakes of snow.

Strange. There were three cars ahead of her and four in back. It seemed like an unusual amount of traffic for this quiet residential neighborhood.

She pulled to the curb and flipped on the overhead map light to read the address she'd hastily scrawled across the paper. She figured once she located Benderman's street, she couldn't miss his house.

It would be the one lit up like a Christmas forest in Disneyland.

When she pulled back onto the street, her headlights immediately lit the sign on Benderman's street. Darby turned abruptly, almost bumping into a car that had stopped directly in her path. Glancing into the rearview mirror, she saw a line of cars following her.

"Mercy," she muttered, "Callahan Tunnel at rush hour."

Inching her way behind the other motorists, she tapped her fingers on the wheel and watched the digital clock tick off the minutes.

There were parked cars lined bumper to bumper down the quiet street, and a steady stream of drivers tried to make their way down the narrow lane. She realized that she had located Cordell Benderman's house.

The atmosphere was complete chaos. There

were so many people on the sidewalks, young couples carrying toddlers trampling through the neighboring lawns to get a closer look. Preschoolers shrieked and squealed with delight when they spotted the live cattle, sheep, and donkeys staked out on the lawn, contentedly munching hay as they watched the circuslike atmosphere with detached indifference.

After waiting fifteen minutes, the miracle Darby had been hoping for finally occurred. A car pulled out in front of her, vacating a parking place.

After backing the BMW into the tight space, she got out and locked the car. For a full three blocks ahead of her, she could see a bright glow against the dark sky.

Amazed, Darby felt herself jostled along with the steady stream of spectators tramping toward the colorful display. When the oohs and aahs grew pronounced, Darby's footsteps slowed. When Cordell Benderman's house finally came into full view, she was as excited as any of the children.

Strains of "Silent Night" accompanied the lowing cows and sheep munching on strands of hay. Behind the animals were wooden figures of Mary and Joseph and the newborn babe, and shepherds kneeling. Above all the figures a bright, glowing star illuminated the lowly stable.

Darby moved on in front of a large, red sleigh. It was loaded with gaily wrapped packages. Santa was ho-ho-hoing in a booming voice to Dasher,

Dancer, Prancer, Vixen, Comet, Cupid, Donner, Blitzen—and Rudolph. Darby smiled as she viewed the comical reindeer. Rudolph was sporting the biggest, reddest, glowingest nose that she'd ever seen. A finer reindeer the world had never seen.

And the world could see it a block away.

There was also an assortment of wooden carolers on the lawn, serenading the onlookers from loudspeakers with a rousing rendition of "Deck the Halls."

The next grouping was of motorized figures of Disney cartoon animals skating about on an icy pond, whirling and dipping up and down to a jazzy version of "Winter Wonderland." Donald, Minnie, Goofy, and Pluto had fixed smiles on their faces as they whizzed around the perimeter of the icy pond. Cinderella, with an ethereal smile on her wooden face, was waltzing with Prince Charming, while Snow White and the seven dwarfs were playing ring-around-the-rosy.

Then there was Santa's workshop with Santa's elves, dressed in bright red and green. Darby found herself growing excited along with the crowd as a rotund, very merry-looking Santa stepped out of the garage. With a dramatic, audible groan, he hoisted a huge sack onto his back and began making his way through the crowd.

The children screamed with delight as he began handing out bright red-and-green peppermint sticks. He patted each child's cheek, asking them to please leave oat-bran cookies and skim milk for him on Christmas Eve.

When he reached Darby, Santa suddenly came to a halt. Setting his sack down in front of her, he leaned back to study her.

"*Ho, ho, ho!*" he said. "Well, well, what *have* we here?"

Darby blushed as he leaned over and reached into his sack, drawing out a large candy cane with a colorful ribbon tied around it.

He offered the treat to Darby, but hurriedly drew it back when she reached.

"Not so fast little girl! Ole Santy needs a little kiss!" he boomed.

Blushing, Darby decided to go along with the game for the benefit of the little ones watching the exchange with wide-eyed innocence.

"Well, sure, Santy." Darby leaned forward to give the jolly old man a peck on the cheek.

But the jolly old man avoided her benign gesture and turned his head so the kiss landed on his warm lips.

Darby's eyes widened as the kiss suddenly took on a personal nature. Jerking back, she stared at him, aghast.

"*Ho, ho, ho!*" Santa patted his padded stomach contentedly, obviously pleased with her reaction. His eyes twinkled merrily as he gazed back at Darby. "Have you been a *good* little girl?"

Too shocked to say what she really thought of

his behavior, Darby dipped her head demurely. "The very best, Santa."

"You're sure now?" Santa reached into his sack and drew out a long piece of paper and began to scan the row upon row of names written upon it. "Now, let me see. What is your name, little girl?"

"Darby."

Santa looked at her again, and for just the briefest of moments Darby could have sworn she'd seen those blue eyes somewhere before.

"*Darby?*" he boomed.

"Yes, sir, Santa."

"Darby what, little girl?"

"Darby Piper, Santa. Surely you have my name on your list!" Darby grinned, glancing at the children in the crowd, who were absolutely enthralled.

"Darby Piper?" Santa shook his head, scanning his list again. "No, I don't believe your name is on my list." He glanced up, his eyes twinkling devilishly now. "You must have been a *bad* little girl."

He handed the large candy cane to the child standing beside Darby.

"*Ho, ho, ho!*" Patting his stomach again, Santa moved on through the crowd, leaving Darby staring after him, dumbfounded.

The incident still puzzled Darby the next morning.

At ten o'clock, Gail ushered in the first appointment: Louis and Arvilla Kinnits. Louis and Arvilla were the spokespersons for the plaintiffs in the "Santa Claus Caper": *Haven Heights* v. *Benderman.*

"Now, Miss Piper, we don't want to stir up a lot of unwarranted trouble," Louis Kinnits explained once they had been comfortably seated. "We just don't see any other way to handle the matter. It's not that we don't like Christmas, we do. And there's not a one of us on the street wants to be a Scrooge. We want you to understand that."

"Yes, you must understand that," Arvilla repeated.

"I understand." Darby remembered how it had taken an hour for her to get out of Benderman's subdivision the previous evening.

"We don't want to make trouble for Mr. Benderman," Arvilla said, "but it's just a mess out there, Ms. Piper. Simply a mess. Benderman's simply going to have to take his decorations down. Our privacy is being violated."

"That's what we'll be asking the court," Darby said.

"Every last twinkling light and figure," Louis added.

"And right away." Arvilla leaned forward. "We don't want this going on until New Year's, you know. I just can't have it. The traffic is simply intolerable."

Louis patted his wife's hand consolingly.

"Once the case is decided, it will be up to the judge to stipulate a time when Mr. Benderman must remove the display," Darby said. "But we will be asking that the decorations be removed as soon as possible." She glanced up. "I must warn you, though, the case may not be heard until after the holidays."

Louis and Arvilla exchanged pained expressions.

"Isn't there any way you can hurry things along?" Louis asked.

"I'm afraid not, Mr. Kinnits. I don't set the court docket."

"Well—" Arvilla rose, picking up her large handbag—"it's simply ruining my holiday."

As she walked her clients to the door, Darby apologized, "I'm sorry, the wheels of justice move slowly at times."

Arvilla sniffed. "Well, if you ask me, the system simply stinks."

"Now, Arvilla," Louis chided, "don't go getting yourself all worked into a stew. Ms. Piper seems quite capable. I'm sure we'll have no trouble at all winning our case."

"I hope not," Arvilla said.

Closing the door to her office a few moments later, Darby leaned against it and heaved a long sigh.

Personally, she was finding this case to be a headache.

Three

Monday morning dawned bright and clear. A skift of snow was scattered across the drive as Darby left for work.

Eyeing the ever-present growling machines resentfully, she noticed that the construction workers had turned the quiet cul-de-sac into a parking lot for heavy equipment.

The men were hunkered around their machines this morning, drinking coffee and shooting the breeze.

Of course, the arrogant one was present. He seemed to have some authority with the crew. At least, she thought, he was strutting around trying to *look* important, whether he actually was or not.

When the man spotted her, he lifted his fore-finger to his hard hat politely.

She turned her back, pointedly ignoring him, and climbed into her car.

Just as the men were tossing out the remains from their foam coffee cups and climbing aboard their big machines, Darby was fastening her seat belt. She glanced at the dash of the BMW as eight o'clock flashed on the clock.

Seconds later, the cul-de-sac sounded like Logan Airport's main runways at rush hour.

Glancing into her rearview mirror, Darby saw that one of the dozers had backed into her drive. The machine was idling now and the cab was empty, the driver having driven there and disap-peared within a matter of moments. "Wouldn't you know it?" she seethed, slapping her hand on the steering wheel irritably.

She climbed out of her car and picked her way down her driveway.

The "patronizing one" was leaning against the side of a pickup, talking to the driver.

Cupping her hands to her mouth, she called, "Excuse me!"

The man glanced up, but his conversation never slackened.

"Excuse me!" she said a little louder this time.

Turning his head, the man gave her an annoyed glance. "Are you talking to me?"

Irritation flooded her. *Was she talking to him?*

He knew very well that she was talking to him! Who else would leave a bulldozer blocking her drive?

"Yes, I'm talking to you." She forced civility back into her voice. He was not going to start her day off wrong again. He was not. "Would you move your dozer so that I may back my car out of my drive?"

"Just keep your britches on." He turned back to the other worker and calmly went on with his conversation.

Keep my britches on? Darby shot him a look of disbelief. *It will be a cold day in Hades before a man like you would coax the "britches" off me,* she fumed.

'If you'll take care of that for me, Mac, I'd appreciate it."

"Sure thing, boss."

As the pickup drove off, the man turned and walked toward Darby. "What's your problem this morning," he asked curtly.

"Same problem it's been every morning you're around here. Your machine is blocking my drive."

He turned his head, his eyes surveying the opening between the dozer and a line of shrubs. "You can't get through a hole *that size*?" he asked incredulously. "You sure you have a license?"

Determined not to stand in muck up to her ankles to argue with him, Darby repeated tightly, "I want that machine out of my way, immediately."

She tried to be her most intimidating, desperately ignoring the provocative scent of his aftershave, but it wasn't easy. She was appalled to realize that nothing about the man was easy to ignore.

"I'll move it just as soon as I can," he said.

Turning, she started slogging back up the drive with as much dignity as her rubber galoshes would allow. She knew better than to push him any further.

The dozer's engine obediently roared to life a moment later, but it seemed to Darby that the man was taking an extraordinarily long time to move the darned thing.

She backed out of her drive, carefully maneuvering the BMW past the dozer.

"Excuse me!" he called down.

When she didn't look up, he gave a sharp piercing whistle.

Darby rolled down her window, frowning. "What?"

"How about having dinner with me tonight?" he shouted above the roar of the big machine.

"How about 'don't make me laugh,' " she shouted back.

As she rushed into Judge Moorhouse's courtroom forty minutes later, she was still appalled at his audacity. *Have dinner with him?* He had to be kidding. Yet she suspected that most women would jump at the chance to spend an evening with him. There was something about the man—

She sagged with relief as she heard the clerk just calling her case number. She was on time. Drawing a deep breath, she tried to steady her frayed nerves.

Still smarting over the run-in, she marched to her table and slapped her briefcase down onto it more solidly than she'd intended. Her client looked at her anxiously.

A hushed silence fell over the courtroom as Judge Moorhouse rapped his gavel, then peered pretentiously over the rim of his glasses at the new arrival.

"Ms. Piper," he intoned placidly.

Darby came to her feet. "Your Honor?"

"So glad you've decided to grace us with your presence this morning. And right on time." Lifting the sleeve of his robe, the judge consulted his watch. "Yes," he mused. "And not a minute to spare, I see."

Blushing, Darby could feel the plaintiff's attorney smirking at her from his seat at the next table. "Yes, sir, Your Honor."

Bill Moorhouse's earlier reprimand still rang in her ears. *Don't be late, again.*

Judge Moorhouse removed his glasses wearily. "Would I be hoping for too much if I asked that we begin now?"

"No, sir, counsel for the defense is ready, Your Honor," Darby murmured.

Dan Middleton rose, sending Darby an amused grin. "The plaintiff is ready, Your Honor."

Taking her seat, Darby shot Dan a smug look. They'd see who was laughing by the end of the day.

It was snowing again when Darby came out of the courthouse late that afternoon. Her head was splitting. The case she was representing was long and tedious, requiring hours and hours of boring, repetitive testimony. She was sure that half the jury had snoozed through the last hour and a half.

Her head was throbbing by the time she'd made her way through rush-hour traffic and stopped by the market for cat food and a frozen dinner.

Wheeling onto her dead-end street, she saw that the construction crew had parked their equipment for the day—directly in her way again.

Inching her car into her drive, she winced as she heard the bumper scrape against the oversize wheels of a crane. Holding her breath, she eased past the machine, mentally cursing an entire generation of construction workers.

She was going to call the general office again tomorrow morning and demand to speak to whoever was responsible for this crew. She was going to complain about the whole ill-mannered lot!

On Tuesday, Darby came out of her house and found the dozer sitting in her drive again. Three men were standing around the machine, hands in their pockets, looking at the back wheel.

Letting the storm door slam shut behind her, she trudged out to the dozer.

Her nemesis glanced up, frowning when he saw her marching determinedly toward him.

"Is my drive the *only* parking place you can find for this thing?" she demanded.

"Have you changed your mind about having dinner with me?" he asked.

"Give me fifty years."

"Tsk, tsk, tsk. Did we get up on the wrong side of the bed?"

She met his amused gaze. "*Move* the dozer," she enunciated tersely.

The man smiled. "There's a small problem with the track. If you'll back off, I'll have it out of your way in a few minutes. Okay?"

No, it *wasn't* okay. He had delayed her every single morning this week, and she was beginning to suspect he was playing some sort of annoying game with her.

She took a deep breath, pursed her lips together,

and watched impatiently as the men stood, hands in their pockets, staring at the wheel.

The arrogant one finally glanced up again, surprise seeping into his handsome features when he saw that she was still standing there. "You need something?"

"I *need* to get out of my drive." It looked to Darby as if the men planned to spend the whole day, hands in their pockets, eyes fixed on the broken track.

"It shouldn't be long," he said, looking away again.

"How *long*?"

"Lady"—the man's patience was clearly coming to an end—"when I know how long, you'll know how long."

Whirling, Darby marched back to the house to call Judge Moorhouse's clerk, vowing to have one construction worker's head on a platter by nightfall.

"Ms. Piper, Ms. Piper, Ms. Piper."

Darby stood repentantly before Judge Moorhouse's bench two hours later.

Bill Moorhouse shook his head in disbelief. "Are you *trying* to upset me?"

"No, sir, Your Honor. You see—"

"Now there," he cut in, "there's the crux of the whole problem. I *do* want to see. You. In court.

On time. Every morning." Judge Moorhouse removed his glasses and began to wipe at an imaginary spec on the lens with his handkerchief. "Do I make myself perfectly clear, Counsel?"

"Yes, sir."

"Crystal clear!" he boomed.

"Yes, sir!"

By the time court recessed at four, Darby's nerves were strung tight. The defense attorney's continual tardiness had become the joke of the court. The spectators snickered most of the morning, and Dan had even quit trying to hide his amusement.

She was the butt of unamusing ridicule, and it was all that construction man's fault!

Driving home, she listened to a tape of Christmas music, hoping to improve her disposition. Somewhere between "Little Drummer Boy" and "I Heard the Bells on Christmas Day," she could feel the tension beginning to drain out of her. She was making too much out of this. She would set her alarm for an earlier wake-up, and tomorrow morning she would leave the house before seven. That way she'd be gone before the construction workers arrived.

Thinking about them, the arrogant man's handsome face came to mind, and her stomach lurched girlishly. She forced the disturbing image aside and concentrated on turning into her subdivision.

She groaned loudly when she saw that the construction crew was working late. Traffic was backed up for blocks as heavy machinery lumbered back and forth across the road.

The BMW inched its way along the long line. Darby could see that up ahead the flagman was directing the traffic across the busy roadway.

The traffic would suddenly zip along, then come to an abrupt halt.

Zip, halt. Zip, halt.

The pattern went on for over ten minutes before she worked her way to the intersection. Darby muttered under her breath when she got close enough to recognize the flagman.

It was him.

Well, this time he wasn't going to get to her.

The flagman leaned forward, dramatically motioning for the crossing traffic to proceed.

Keeping her eyes fixed straight ahead, Darby let the BMW begin to roll. The first car zipped through the intersection, the second, the third, the fourth. Then as her BMW, the fifth car, picked up speed, suddenly, *up* went the stop sign again.

Darby slammed on the brakes, practically standing the BMW on its nose.

Darn his hide! He had done that deliberately, she seethed. He had been letting ten to twelve cars through the intersection at a time, but when her car had appeared, he'd only let four through. *Four!*

A few minutes later the man let the BMW cross the intersection, waving pleasantly at Darby as she shot past him in a squeal of burning rubber.

The following morning Cody sneezed and reached for another tissue as he flipped over a sheet of blueprints. Glancing at his watch, he snapped open a bottle of antihistamines, dumped two into the palm of his hand, then fumbled for a glass of water.

Lord, his head felt as if Larry Bird had been dribbling it across a basketball court this morning.

The phone rang, and he grabbed it on the second ring as he searched for a crossline on the blueprint.

"C.B. Construction." His voice sounded raspy, and he swallowed, wincing as he felt the tenderness in his throat. What he wouldn't give just to go home and crawl into bed for the day.

"Yes, I want to speak with the owner please?"

"This is he." Cody grinned, recognizing what was now becoming a familiar voice. He shifted the phone to his other ear, preparing to assume a slightly higher-pitched voice.

"I'm sorry, but this is Darby Piper again."

"Yes, ma'am."

"Ordinarily," Darby said, "I would not waste my time calling. I realize it isn't easy to work with the public, but I really have had it up to here with one of your workers."

"Oh? Has *he* been giving you a problem again, Miss Piper?" Cody asked. He hoped his voice sounded properly horrified.

"Yes. The man seems set on annoying me. I think he must be one of your foremen—or at least that's my impression. He seems to be in charge of the men who park their machinery on the cul-de-sac where I live."

"And what's he done this time?"

"He was acting as a flagman yesterday afternoon. And, well, he made me stop, and my car was the very last to go through the intersection."

"Honestly?"

"Yes. The man has caused me to be late for work twice this week, and I *insist* that you do something about him."

"Well—I just can't imagine—what was your name again?" Cody prompted indignantly.

"Darby Piper!"

Cody absently reached for another tissue. "I am sorry the man keeps annoying you, Ms. Piper. I've had one of my foremen speak to him about the matter, but the man seems to think that it's you, provoking him."

"Me? Why the nerve—I haven't done anyt'   '"

Darby carried the phone to her window to control her irritation. Below her, she the Marketplace crowded with shop' arms filled with bundles and gaily wrapped Christmas presents. "He deliberately antagonizes me!"

"Well, I'll certainly have my foreman speak to him again—what street did you say you live on?"

Irritated, Darby told him her address again. "Because of this man's arrogance, I'm out a towing charge, two pairs of hose, and a pair of new pumps."

"Oh, I *am* sorry to hear that. If you'll just send the bill to me, I'll see that it's taken care of."

Cody blew his nose.

"Pardon?"

"I said if you would send the—"

"Oh, I fully intend to send you the bill," Darby assured him.

"And if you want to buy another couple of pair of hose and some new blue shoes, send that bill to me, too," he added nicely.

"Thank you." Now here was a considerate man, Darby thought. It was too bad he wasn't more insightful about the men he employed.

On the other end of the phone, Cody leaned back in his chair, grinning. Was *she* going to be hot under the collar when she discovered who she was talking to! His grin widened devilishly. There was something about the little spitfire that he found stimulating. He had to admit he liked to ruffle her feathers. Or maybe he just liked the way her face turned a rosy shade of pink, or the spirit he saw in her eyes when he was annoying her.

He would readily admit that he liked a woman with spirit, and he would bet Darby Piper had plenty of it—in and out of bed.

He suddenly found himself wanting to test the theory.

But he needed to let up on her. He had worked long and hard to build a good reputation for C.B. Construction, and he wasn't going to spoil it by continuing to annoy an attorney. . . .

"Are you still there?" Darby asked after the silence stretched out.

"Yes, ma'am. I apologize again for the inconvenience. You realize the crew is under a great deal of pressure? Winter is setting in, and we're under contract to have several miles of pipe laid before the ground gets too hard. Every day we go over our deadline costs money. I'm sure the man—a foreman you say?"

"Well, actually I don't know that. He might be just a flunky."

"Yes—probably just a flunky," he agreed dryly. "Don't worry, ma'am. I'll personally ream him out."

"Thank you. I hope it won't be necessary to bother you again."

"I hope not too—at least concerning such an unpleasant subject."

"Thank you."

"You're welcome."

Cody hung up a moment later, snickering.

Darby hung up, smiling smugly. She would

love to be there when the *owner* of the construction company collared that fool. He deserved whatever was coming to him.

Yawning, she savored the idea of sleeping in another hour tomorrow morning. Now that the dozer wouldn't be blocking her drive, she could resume her normal schedule.

Turning back to her desk, she suddenly froze, staring off into thin air.How in the world did the owner of C.B. Construction know that she needed to replace *blue* pumps?

Four

That afternoon, two dozen red roses and three pair of silk stockings were delivered to Darby's office.

"You and Prince Rainier are perhaps going together now?" Gail teased as she handed the gifts to Darby.

Darby frowned, reaching for the card. "If we are, the prince hasn't mentioned it." She smiled as she read the brief message:

The dozer operator and C.B. Construction send their heartfelt apologies.

"Well, how nice," Darby said, beaming.

She admired the budding roses. The owner of C.B. Construction was one man who knew how to treat a woman.

*　　*　　*

Wednesday morning Darby was in her office a few minutes before seven. She wanted at least two hours to go over her notes on the Benderman case before Louis and Arvilla Kinnits arrived.

Her intercom buzzed at precisely nine A.M.

"Yes?"

"The Kinnitses are here."

"Thanks," Darby said, setting aside her coffee cup. She stood and smiled as Louis and Arvilla entered the office.

"Good morning."

"It's simply too cold for me," Arvilla sniffed.

"Now, dear, I told you to wear your heavy coat," Louis fussed.

"I don't like that coat, Louis." Arvilla's tone suggested that that was that and she didn't want to hear any more about her heavy coat.

The Kinnitses took their seats and waited for Darby to begin.

Reseating herself, Darby folded her hands. "Would you care for coffee?"

"No," Arvilla sniffed again, "it gives me heartburn."

"Louis?"

Louis glanced at Arvilla expectantly, and Arvilla shook her head.

"No . . . thank you," he said.

"You understand that we're not going to change

our position, so just exactly why are we having this meeting?" Arvilla asked.

Darby moved a stack of files aside, choosing her words carefully. "I wanted to discuss a possibility with you before Mr. Benderman and his attorney arrive."

"What possibility?" Louis asked.

"I was wondering if you and your neighbors would consider a compromise." Darby had slept little the night before. The Benderman case bothered her. She could readily sympathize with her clients, but she wondered if there wasn't a better way to settle the dispute than having it heard before a judge. It was clear to her that Cordell Benderman loved children and that he meant no harm by displaying his elaborate Christmas scene.

Surely with a little ingenuity the case could be handled out of court.

"Compromise?" Arvilla edged forward on her chair. "Certainly not. That display comes down, and the sooner the better."

"I see," Darby said, choosing her next words just as carefully. "I just thought that someone with your capacity for compassion might find spending Christmas Eve in court unpalatable." Darby smiled pleasantly.

"Christmas Eve?" Louis prompted.

"Yes. That's our court date."

Louis glanced at Arvilla.

Arvilla shook her head warningly.

"The whole point of this suit is to have the display removed. I thought with a bit of resourcefulness on our part we might spare you and your neighbors the unpleasantness of a court battle." Darby edged forward. "Perhaps you would like to reconsider a compromise?"

"Oh, I don't think so," Louis began, then paused, frowning, "Christmas Eve, you say?"

"Yes . . . why don't you go home, talk it over with your neighbors—perhaps together we can come up with a few minor concessions—"

"Absolutely not," Arvilla stated emphatically.

"But dear . . . the office party is on Christmas Eve . . . it won't look good if I miss it," Louis offered meekly.

"Tough, Louis."

Louis shrugged lamely. "Absolutely not. No compromise," he agreed.

Sighing, Darby picked up the files with her notes. "Then shall we get down to business?"

At exactly nine-thirty, Darby along with Louis and Arvilla walked down the hall to the conference room.

"Your office is a little plain compared to this, isn't it?" Arvilla asked, eyeing the festive, gaily decorated reception area.

"A little," Darby agreed, thinking about the one sprig of mistletoe Dan had tacked on her door.

Each year the firm put up a mammoth Christmas tree in the lobby. Wreaths and mistletoe adorned every office door, and almost every day one of the secretaries brought in some sinfully delicious home-baked goods. The Christmas spirit had definitely invaded the very proper offices of Yates, Bates, Slag & Choleric.

Darby opened the door of the conference room and followed her clients inside.

Jeff McDonald stood, and Darby accepted his extended hand.

"Darby."

"Jeffrey."

Jeff and Darby had been classmates in law school.

"Ms. Piper, I'd like you to meet my client, Cordell Benderman," Jeff said.

The smile on Darby's face died as the tall man sitting behind Jeff stood up.

As she stifled a groan, her distressed eyes locked with Cody Benderman's.

"Mr. Benderman owns and operates C.B. Construction," Jeff continued. "Cody tells me they've been installing sewer lines in your subdivision, Darby. He says he's seen you around the area."

Darby's face flamed. The conceited, insufferable jerk! She wanted to crawl in a hole. Not only was Benderman the dozer operator, he *owned* the construction company! She had been talking to *him* the day she'd called and complained about the dozer blocking her drive. The lovely flowers and—hose—had come from him. And the kiss! The one from Santa that she'd practically enjoyed. It was all him.

"Mr. Benderman," Darby returned curtly.

Cody nodded, amusement flickering in his eyes. "Ms. Piper."

Jeff turned to pour himself a cup of coffee, and the Kinnitses were already seated, leaving Cody and Darby alone for a moment.

"I didn't recognize you without your bulldozer," Darby said under her breath.

"Oh? Well, I'd recognize you anywhere," Cody said calmly.

Oh, she just bet he would. And she'd also bet he'd had a good laugh at her irate phone calls!

Turning her back on him, she walked over and took her chair. She struggled to control her temper. She was going to be her most professional self.

"Shall we begin, gentlemen?" she asked crisply.

Jeff glanced up, surprised by the sudden note of hostility in her voice. "Uh . . . sure." He quickly returned to his seat beside Benderman. "Let's see now." Jeff opened his notes, his eyes scanning the yellow legal pad.

Darby kept her eyes on her notes, determined to ignore Cordell Benderman. He sat across from her, dressed in a well-tailored suit that fit his broad shoulders with disgusting perfection. She could feel his blue-eyed gaze studying her.

She'd known he was good-looking, but dressed in a gray suit and minus his hard hat, he was awesome. And he knew it. She was sure of that. He emanated the air of a man who got what he wanted—when he wanted it.

Well, if he thought he could charm her, he was wrong. And if he thought he could charm Arvilla, he was just plain bananas.

His cocky little half-smile wouldn't faze Arvilla Kinnits.

Squirming on her chair, Darby caught Cody watching her again, and she forced herself to sit perfectly still. Did he know she was wearing the stockings he'd sent her? She hoped not. Belatedly she realized that the stockings had been too intimate a gift. She should have sent them back, but at the time it had been such a nice gesture, and such a unique apology, that she'd kept them. Now the hose suddenly seemed to be touching her legs in an obscenely intimate way. She began to squirm again.

Jeff's voice interrupted her thoughts. "First, my client would like to express his dismay over this unfortunate suit." Leaning back on his chair, Jeff folded his hands genially, focusing his attention now on Arvilla and Louis. "Mr. Benderman has no ill will toward his neighbors," he said in the nicest of voices. "On the contrary. My client considers his Christmas display a way of expressing his goodwill, his faith, and his Christmas spirit to his neighbors—and mankind, if you will. Cordell Benderman has put a lot of time, effort, love, and yes, money into that display. He is sincerely sorry for the traffic congestion his generosity has caused, but he respectfully suggests to the plaintiffs that the season comes but once a year." Jeff's features turned woeful as he gazed at the Kinnitses.

"Surely," Jeff concluded, "we can reach an amicable solution to our problem without taking this to court."

A long, meaningful silence followed as the defense attorney allowed time for his suggestion to take root.

Clearing her throat, Darby picked up her notes. "My clients will agree that Mr. Benderman has a very complex display," she said. "But one does wonder why Mr. Benderman couldn't have created something a bit simpler for the enjoyment of his family."

"Mr. Benderman is single," Jeff said.

I can believe that, Darby thought. *He's arrogant, presumptuous, overbearing, with an ego that would swallow half of Boston. But thank God he's not married—Darby! It would be even worse if she'd harbored her idiotic, romantic thoughts about a married man!*

"My client simply loves children," Jeff explained

in a paternal voice. "His display is solely for the enjoyment of the little ones, and he has no desire to cause his neighbors problems."

"Yet, there is a problem," Darby said, "and the problem is that the display creates a public nuisance."

"My client is aware of the complaint."

"What your client is apparently not aware of, Jeff, is that my clients have had their yards trampled, their peace broken, and their own Christmas spirit intruded upon by a constant stream of strangers. Your client has chosen to ignore their complaints year after year; indeed, he has expanded the chaos each season."

"My client respectfully apologizes and reminds his neighbors that he will be happy to remove the display early this year. Say"—Jeff glanced at Benderman—"the day after Christmas?"

Cody smiled pleasantly at Arvilla. "I think that can be arranged if Mr. and Mrs. Kinnits agree."

Arvilla flushed, openly melting under Benderman's blue-eyed gaze. "Well . . . we could talk to the others—"

Seeing that Arvilla was about to buckle in the face of Benderman's charm, Darby tossed her notes into her folder and stood. "My clients find that unacceptable. The display comes down immediately, or we go to court."

"Oh, my . . ." Arvilla said, her hand coming up

to straighten her hair primly. She smiled back at Cody. "Should we be so hasty . . . ?"

Darby shot Louis a foreboding look.

"Now dear . . . don't you think you should let Ms. Piper handle this?"

With a frown Arvilla retreated, but Darby could see that she was obviously smitten with the handsome construction owner. "Well . . . I wouldn't *mind* talking to a few . . ."

"Darby, you know the court date is set for Christmas Eve," Jeff said. Leaning over, he whispered, "You don't want to make us spend the *whole* day in court."

"No, I don't. Perhaps your client would consider dismantling the display earlier?" she whispered back.

Darby steadfastly refused to meet Cody's gaze.

"My client would find that unacceptable," Jeff argued. "Come on, Darby"—he leaned closer, his voice lowering and growing more anxious—"Benderman has a perfect right to do what he wants on his property!"

Darby held her ground. "Then I guess we will not be baking pumpkin pies on Christmas Eve."

Jeff muttered something under his breath, then stood, glancing at Cody.

Cody shrugged his broad shoulders vaguely.

Jeff closed his briefcase and rose to walk out of the conference room with Benderman a moment later.

"What's that supposed to mean?" Arvilla asked.

"It means they're not willing to compromise," Darby said. She was irritated with herself for not being able to remain more objective about Cody Benderman. "We're going to court."

"But"—Louis peered at Darby expectantly—"I thought you *wanted* to compromise?"

Walking out of the conference room with the Kinnitses, Darby shot a reproachful look at Cordell Benderman's wide set of shoulders as they disappeared down the corridor. "Compromise?" Her eyes narrowed. "Where did you ever get that idea?"

"Ms. Piper?"

Darby was coming out of her office building late that afternoon, at close to six-thirty, exiting the revolving doors onto the busy street. She glanced up at the sound of a man's voice calling her name. She frowned as she saw Cordell Benderman striding toward her.

Turning up the collar of her coat, she set off toward the parking garage as he fell into step beside her.

"We need to talk."

"I believe we already have."

Recognizing the tone of mockery in her voice, Cody shrugged. "I know I should have told you who I was when you called the office the other day."

"But you didn't."

"No, it was too good an opportunity to get you back," he admitted.

"Well, congratulations. I'm sure you had a good laugh."

"Yeah." He shook his head, grinning. "It was great."

Ignoring his attempt at humor, Darby huddled deeper inside her coat as they threaded their way through the crowded streets. She found herself walking shoulder to shoulder beside him, and she wondered why the innocent contact should feel so electrifying. She couldn't remember when she had been aware of a man.

"Could I interest you in a drink?" he asked.

"No, thank you."

"Ah, come on, Ms. Piper. Lighten up. I think we should talk this thing out, try to come to an agreeable solution."

"Concerning what?"

"Concerning whether or not we should start dating."

Darby glanced up, stunned. "Dating?"

"Yeah, you're beginning to get to me."

Darby averted her gaze, walking faster now. "If it bothers you that I'm representing the plaintiffs, then I suggest you talk to your attorney." They paused at the corner, waiting for the light to change.

"That's not what I meant. I'm not concerned about your being biased against my case. I know that you are. I just find you attractive, and I think we should get to know each other outside the realm of business."

"I never mix business with pleasure, Mr. Benderman."

He glanced down at her. The top of her head almost came to his shoulders. "I would've bet my last dime on that."

"And as for our relationship, you keep your dozer out of my drive, and I won't be calling you—to complain about you."

The light changed, and they were swept along with the throng of Christmas shoppers.

"But you won't go out with me?"

"That's right."

"Too bad. I think you're missing a great opportunity. You get the stockings?"

Darby felt her cheeks coloring. She was acutely aware of the taupe silk stockings hugging her legs.

"If I'd known you had sent them—"

"You would have sent them back."

"Yes."

"You didn't like them?"

"That isn't the point."

They crossed another street and walked on.

"I don't guess it would help if I apologized for my actions and admitted that I've been a jerk?"

An unbidden smile threatened to mar Darby's bad mood. The man was impossible, yet she had to admit that he sparked a responsive cord in her, one that she found dangerous. She wasn't sure she liked anything *about* Cody Benderman, but she was beginning to fear she liked *him* too much. "I'm not sure, why don't you try?"

"And have you laugh in my face?" he said.

"It's possible."

They turned the corner and made their way up the ramp to the aboveground parking garage. The cold wind whistled through the concrete openings. Hurrying to her car, Darby unlocked the door.

Cody suddenly reached out to hold the door closed.

Darby glanced up, and their eyes met. The strangest tingle began somewhere in the pit of her stomach and spiraled up through her like warm, red wine.

"Sure you won't change your mind about having that drink, Ms. Piper?"

Meeting his gaze evenly, Darby fortified her resistance. It would be unthinkable to socialize with him, even though she had to admit that the thought was tempting. "I'm quite sure, Mr. Benderman."

His gaze ran over her lazily. "A pity. I like a woman with your spirit."

"Really?" She smiled. "And I would have sworn you liked all women."

A grin played at the corner of the handsome rascal's mouth. "Well, you would have been wrong. I'm pretty selective about my women."

Brushing his hand away from the door, she got into her car. She turned the ignition, causing the engine to roar to life, and a moment later she backed out of her parking space.

"Hey!" Cody called. "I don't give up easily. We may have just stumbled on something big—hey, I want to see you again!"

Rolling down her window, Darby stuck her head out and called back, "You will. In court, on Christmas Eve!"

She drove off, almost regretting that she hadn't taken him up on his offer to have a drink. Almost.

On Thursday evening Darby had just sat down in front of her television to eat a bowl of clam chowder when Cody's face suddenly flashed on the screen. Frowning, she quickly turned up the volume.

"No, ma'am, I can't understand it. Christmas is a time for children. A time for love and sharing."

A young reporter, her long, dark hair tossing in the wind, was interviewing Benderman. Cody was standing in his front yard, surrounded by his wooden shepherds and a live camel.

Darby's spoon clattered to the counter. *A live camel!* He'd added a live camel to the chaos!

She sat in shock, watching as the interview continued.

"Mr. Benderman, we understand that your neighbors have filed a class action suit against you, *demanding* that you remove this display. Is that correct?"

"Yes, ma'am. They've decided that I can't have my manger scene or my angels or my Christmas carols."

Darby could see the interviewer's face begin to soften with sympathy, and she felt her temper rising. Exactly *what* was Benderman trying to pull this time?

"And I have to go to court on Christmas Eve," he told the viewers, looking straight into the camera now. "If Ms. Piper has her way, I'll have to tear down my decorations and never put them up again. Now, does that sound fair to you? Do you think that is the way to show the true spirit of Christmas?" He sighed. "Well, all I can say is, people ought to stand up for their rights or next thing we know they'll be trying to put a ban on Christmas trees."

Darby seethed.

Turning back to the camera, the reporter's face

sobered. "So there you have the story of how the Grinch is trying to steal Christmas. Cordell Benderman is a local contractor whose Christmas display has become a highly anticipated event in the Boston area. Late today I tried to reach the plaintiff's attorney, Darby Piper, with the law firm of Yates, Bates, Slag and Choleric, but Ms. Piper was not available for comment—"

Darby snapped off the television, then began to pace the floor angrily. How could he do that to her? The man had no scruples!

The phone rang a moment later, and she snatched up the receiver impatiently.

"Yes!"

"Darby, Vance Choleric. Did you catch the news on the local channel?"

Darby's heart sank. "Did you?" she asked lamely.

"Darb, this doesn't look good for the firm, public relations—wise."

"I know, Vance. I can't believe Benderman would stoop so low." The case had started out as a relatively simple one. Darby kneaded her temples with her fingertips anxiously. Now it was turning into a nightmare!

"I think we'd better meet in my office first thing in the morning and discuss strategy," Vance suggested. "How's eight-thirty?"

"Eight-thirty's fine, Vance. I'll be there."

Replacing the receiver, Darby hurriedly reached for her bottle of aspirin.

* * *

When Darby entered the offices the next morning, she found Gail and one of the other receptionists taking calls and messages as quickly as the six telephone lines coming into the office allowed.

Darby picked up eight messages, and she crept off toward the coffee machine, filled a foam cup, then edged toward Vance's office.

She was surprised to find Vance, Carter, and a pale-faced Victor Slag waiting for her.

"Darby, come in. Sit down, please," Vance said.

Darby noticed a stack of pink telephone messages piled in front of Vance. Taking a seat quietly, she crossed her hands in her lap and waited.

She had a feeling that Cody Benderman's appearance on the six-o'clock news the night before had something to do with the stack of messages.

"It appears that we have a little problem," Vance cleared his throat, then continued, "Actually, it could turn into a serious problem. The telephones have been ringing off the hook this morning with calls from people upset over Cordell Benderman's plight. Every call we've received has been in favor of Benderman's keeping his display. All of a sudden *we've* become the Grinch who stole Christmas, and the public is hot under the collar about it."

"This firm has been in existence for seventy-five

years," Victor said, "and nothing like this has ever happened. We simply can't have it. None of it—not at all. We have to do something."

Darby glanced up, heartsick at the turn of events. The four partners had never had adverse publicity, and they didn't want any.

Yates, Bates, Slag & Choleric was the most conservative law firm in Boston. The partners wore only gray suits. Their *ties* didn't even have patterns.

Vance turned back to Darby, sober-faced. "Darby, will the neighborhood association accept a compromise?"

"They might have, but I've already received two phone calls from Louis and Arvilla Kinnits this morning. The Kinnitses are spokespersons for their neighborhood. Naturally, they're as upset as we are by Benderman's theatrics. Once again, they're determined to fight this all the way now. Benderman's made his entire neighborhood look like a bunch of heartless scrooges."

"Then perhaps we should put someone else on the case," Victor prompted. "Perhaps one of us—"

"No!" Darby said. "That would only make it look as if we're agreeing with Mr. Benderman, when, according to the law, the neighborhood association has every right to bring suit against him. He *is* treading on their rights, no matter how he tries to slant public sympathy in his direction. If you remove me from the case, we're giving in to his soap-box grandstanding. I don't think that we should do that."

"Darby, it may be the only sensible way to resolve the stalemate," Vance pointed out. "I think I could—"

"The sensible way," Darby objected, "is to beat Mr. Benderman in court. And I can do that."

Vance sighed. "You'd better."

"I can. I have video pictures of his display, of people trampling through yards, the steady flow of traffic, the chaos—plus, I have a great body of legal precedence. We can win this case," Darby said, her resolve firming.

"But do we *want* to win this case?" Slag muttered.

"It's the only way to prove we're not . . . not uncaring Grinches," Darby argued. "If we give in now, we're admitting that Benderman is right. We can't do that to our clients."

"She has a point," Vance said.

"Well, I just don't know," Victor conceded. "It worries me."

"I think we should agree to let it ride for a few days," Carter said calmly. "It might blow over."

Darby relaxed, until Slag spoke up again.

"I still don't like it. This firm has never had a hint of scandal, not in its seventy-five years. I, for one, am not pleased to just sit around and do nothing." His pale eyes pinpointed Darby resentfully. "I'm not pleased at all that this absurdity has happened. It seems clear that this could have been settled out of court. I shall expect to see this matter settled promptly, and with the utmost discretion. No more news conferences, no more public displays, no more bad publicity for the firm. Is that understood, young woman?"

"Yes, sir," Darby replied respectfully.

The meeting broke and Darby stood.

Laying a hand on her shoulder, Carter smiled. "Don't let it upset you. Victor's only concerned about the firm's reputation."

"I know, Carter, and I'll handle the matter with the utmost discretion."

Walking back to her office, Darby only hoped that she could convince Benderman to do the same. Besides being as stubborn as a mule, he didn't have any qualms about creating a circus of publicity. Obviously he didn't mind making a complete fool of her in the process.

Her heart sank. Her shining future was suddenly teetering on the brink of disaster. Whatever happened, she would be blamed for putting the firm in a bad light with the public.

The only way she could hope to salvage her reputation and—if she was lucky—her partnership possibilities was to win the Santa Claus Caper, hands down.

Puddigan's was bursting at the seams when she arrived late that afternoon.

Spotting a small table near the window, Darby made her way across the room, signaling to the waitress that she would have her usual white-wine spritzer.

Slipping out of her coat, she suddenly tensed as she sensed someone standing over her shoulder. As she glanced up, her heart sank. "Oh . . . please," she groaned, "just go away."

Cody grinned, casually pulling up a chair as if he had been invited to join her. "Fancy meeting you here. Care if I join you?"

"Yes," Darby returned evenly.

"Ah, come on. Lighten up. I'm not so bad."

As he placed his chair opposite her, his knee brushed against hers. Darby shot him a warning glance. His innocent contact was becoming too disconcerting.

He smiled, trying to get her to loosen up. "Why don't you want me to sit with you?"

"I consider it fraternizing with the enemy."

"It's not *my* idea to be enemies," he reminded her.

Darby made a disgusted noise in the back of her throat. "Am I hearing right? I thought I was the scourge of Christmas present."

Cody grinned again. He did have the nicest smile. "I think I said 'Grinch,' and I was just playing it up to the press."

"No kidding."

He'd brought his drink with him, and he stared

at the glass for a moment, turning it absently on the table in front of him. "Look, I've been thinking about the case. Isn't there some way we can settle this without going to court?"

Darby leaned forward, running her hand through her hair wearily. "Is that what you really want?"

He lifted his gaze, and their eyes met. There was a crazy ringing in Darby's ears, and she was almost certain it wasn't the Salvation Army bell being rung by the volunteer standing outside the front door.

"That's one of the things I want," he admitted.

Cody studied her. She looked tired, and for the first time he realized how diminutive she was. Somehow he'd thought of her as more threatening the way she'd stomped out to his dozer and demanded he get it out of her way. She had been like a terrier snapping at an elephant, but she had such an authoritative way about her that the elephant had moved.

Now, leaning back on his chair, he gazed at her. Funny, but he'd never really looked at her before. Her hands were long and slim and delicate. Her voice was melodic—when it wasn't demanding that he move his equipment. And she was obviously a pretty damn good attorney or she wouldn't be working for such a prestigious law firm.

Darby glanced up, annoyed that he was staring at her. "What?"

"You're damn cute, Ms. Piper."

"And you're damned annoying, Mr. Benderman."

They looked at each other, and then all of a sudden they both were grinning.

"You honestly think I should take down my display?"

"It doesn't matter what I think," Darby conceded. "My clients believe they have a legitimate complaint."

Leaning forward, his gaze searched hers meaningfully. "But I want to know what you think."

She met his gaze and noticed for the first time how thick his lashes were. A woman would die for those, she thought. And his smile was nice, when he wasn't tormenting her. His hands were square and strong, and his shoulders were broad and well muscled. All in all, Cody Benderman was a splendid male.

"I can see both sides," she confessed.

A slow grin spread across his features. "I knew it. I *knew* if I dug deep enough I'd uncover the real Darby Piper."

She flushed under his softened gaze.

"How about a compromise?" he said.

Darby was still a bit skeptical. "What are you offering?"

He shrugged. "I don't know. But there should be a way around this."

"There is. Take down your display."

He shook his head, smiling at her. "You know I won't do that. At this point it's as much the principle of the thing as the reality of it. I've lived in that housing development since long before most of those houses were built. I keep to myself, mow my lawn regularly, always try to be a good neighbor, and buy more boxes of broken peanut-brittle candy to support the Mighty Mite football team and Little League baseball than you and I could ever hope to eat in a lifetime. I've picked up kids when they've wrecked their bikes and handed out my share of bandages and Kool-Aid. When old man Winters had a flu fire, I was the one who called the fire department. Now, because I have one measly little Christmas display five weeks out of the year, I've become the bogeyman. I don't like it, and I'm not about to knuckle under."

"Isn't that being a little stubborn?"

"Maybe. But I have rights too. And if I'm a good neighbor eleven months out of the year, it seems to me they can put up with my idiosyncrasies for the other one. Is that asking too much?"

"I don't know. It isn't my yard and shrubs that are being trampled."

He grinned, reading her mind. "But you've had to put up with my machinery tearing up your yard and shrubs for the past month, isn't that what you're thinking?"

She had to return his smile this time. "Yes, and

though I've hated every moment of it, it hasn't killed me. I've been cooperative."

"Cooperative?" He threw his head back and hooted.

She knew that he was teasing her now. Humor danced in his eyes, and she had to admit that what she'd just said sounded a little silly after the way she'd acted. "It's a term we lawyers use when we're at a disadvantage," she said.

"Oh. Well, I'm not too up on lawyerese. Why don't you use a little of it to persuade your clients to drop their lawsuit?"

"Afraid you'll lose?"

"Nope. Just don't have the time to hassle with it. I'm two weeks behind in my schedule with this sewer-line construction because of the snow, and you're not helping matters any."

"Me? Why do you keep implying that I'm causing all the trouble?"

His eyes skimmed her leisurely. "You know that red dress you wear?"

Her brows lifted. "The wool one?"

"Hell, I don't know what it's made out of, but it sure shows off your legs." He winked at her again. "I took out a row of shrubs by mistake last week just trying to get a closer look. Nice, Ms. Piper. Real nice. I'd still like to get a closer look."

Darby blushed again. Why was she sitting here falling for his smooth line. "Why are you working with the crew? I'd have thought the management duties would keep you inside."

"They usually do. But one of my best men has been out with health problems. So, I'm filling his place until this job is done. It's hard to find good foremen."

Glancing at her watch, Darby saw that it was getting late. She was surprised to realize that she almost hated to leave. "I'm sorry, I have to go."

"Not half as sorry as I am."

Their gazes met again, then parted reluctantly.

Darby stood and reached for her coat. Cody came to his feet.

"It's been nice talking to you." Cody held out his hand as a peace offering.

She accepted it, and they shook.

"For a Grinch, you're an awfully pretty one," he said.

"I wish you'd mentioned that yesterday when you called the news conference."

"I didn't 'call' that conference. One of the reporters caught me coming out of the house. I was mad as hell after our meeting the other day, and I said more than I should have. Did the press call you?"

"No, but my firm called me. On the carpet. They're not fond of all the negative publicity."

"Sorry. I don't mean to cause trouble."

"No big deal." She shrugged. "I just may get

passed over on my partnership bid because of all this flak."

Cody did feel bad now. "I am sorry—listen, if the promotion doesn't come through, we'll get married. You can forget all about working and devote all your time and energy to taking care of me and our children." A teasing grin spread across his face as he saw her stunned look.

"You'll let me know—about the promotion?"

"You're quite a kidder, aren't you," she said when she'd recovered enough to find her voice.

"Yeah—I hope to hell I am," he murmured to himself. He had to admit that he found her attractive—damned attractive. Dangerously attractive. "Listen—you won't take it personally about this lawsuit, will you?"

Shaking her head, she returned his smile. "No, I won't take it personally."

"Good, because I don't plan to take the display down."

"Why doesn't that surprise me?"

He grinned. "See you later, counselor."

"Yeah," Darby murmured. "Later."

Darby left encouraged by Cody's good mood. She hoped that his sudden change in attitude was an indication that from now on he was willing to play fair with her.

Five

She'd been *wrong* to trust him! Darby thought. *Dead wrong!* Cody Benderman didn't know the meaning of the word *fair*. And just how far Cordell Benderman was willing to go to win his case became even clearer to Darby when she walked out of her office building the next Monday.

Snow was falling again. She wished now that she had been a little less vain and a lot wiser and worn her boots instead of her shoes, which were more dressy than sensible.

Tucking her hair beneath her hat, she started down the steps, dreading the thought of spending the next couple of hours in a crowded mall, but she had little choice. She hadn't bought a single gift yet, and it was nearly the middle of December.

Ahead, she could see a large crowd gathering in front of the office complex. Frowning, she wondered what was going on now.

After shouldering her way through the maze of bodies, she froze.

Cody Benderman, decked out in a Santa Claus suit, was *picketing* Yates, Bates, Slag & Choleric!

He was wearing a gigantic placard reading, DOWN WITH THE GRINCH, except the word *Grinch* was marked out and *Darby Piper* was handwritten in its place.

Fury colored Darby's face. Darn him! Darn that man's rotten hide!

Santa turned, and spotting Darby, he waved.

She shouldered her way angrily through the crowd, calling heatedly, "*What* do you think you're doing?"

"Picketing the law offices of Yates, Bates, Slag & Choleric."

"Well, stop it!"

"No way. This is a public sidewalk."

"Then get *my* name off that sign!" Darby ordered, oblivious of the amused chortles beginning to break out in the crowd.

When Darby reached Cody, they stood nose to nose.

"I don't suppose that you would consider having dinner with me when I'm finished?" he asked hopefully.

"Not on your life. You take that sign down right now!"

"Aww, come on, Darb, you know I can't do that. I have my rights too," he protested.

Glancing over her shoulder anxiously, Darby remembered where they were. She lowered her voice. "Cody, please, this is serious. You're ruining my career." She heard herself begging, but she didn't care. She had to get him away from the building before one of the senior partners saw him.

"Hey, that turns me on." Serious blue eyes met distraught brown ones.

"What? To hear me beg?" she exclaimed.

"No, for you to call me Cody instead of Benderman." He smiled at her, a nice warm smile that tied her stomach in knots.

For a long moment their gazes held. *Careful, Darby, he could so easily lure you away,* she thought, then quickly shook the disturbing thought aside.

"Why are doing this to me?"

"Look, I told you not to take this personally— and you agreed that you wouldn't," he said. "And now look. You're coming all unglued. This is just business."

"Cody, please." Darby glanced over her shoulder again at the swelling crowd. "I've worked hard to get where I am. I *worked* my way through law school waiting tables and cleaning houses. I haven't had anything handed to me. Becoming a senior partner with a top-notch law firm is all I ever wanted, and now you're about to tear down everything I've worked so hard for the past three years."

"Well, you see, I've been thinking about that." He lowered the placard. "I know you have your job, and I have mine, but I can't see any reason why that has to interfere with you and I beginning a personal relationship."

She stared back at him as if he had completely lost his mind. "Are you serious?"

"You bet your sweet life I'm serious." His gaze softened. "Hey, look. I like you, okay? And I have just enough male ego to think that you might be feeling the same way about me. Now I'm aware that we've gotten off on the wrong foot, and I'm aware we've got this silly lawsuit standing in our way, but I'm willing to take my chances that we'll be able to work our way through these trivial obstacles."

"*Trivial* obstacles?" she asked incredulously. Darby willed her erratic heartbeat to slow down. "Cody, this is absolutely crazy—I can't become personally involved with you!"

"Why not?" Cody was aware that the crowd was watching them. They were creating quite a spectacle, but at the moment he didn't give a damn. "Are you involved with someone else?"

"No—"

He sagged with relief. "Good."

"Are you?" she found herself asking lamely. He had the *bluest*, most compelling eyes she'd ever gazed into.

"No, ma'am, but all of a sudden I don't find the idea all that disagreeable."

"Cody, even if I wanted to, I can't get involved with you . . . it wouldn't be professional."

His gaze grew more determined. "There's only one way I'll leave."

It was she who sagged this time. Sickly. "I have a feeling I don't want to hear this."

"Have dinner with me."

Her eyes opened again. "That's blackmail!"

He shrugged. "Those are my terms, counselor. Take it or leave it."

"Cody Benderman!" She stamped her foot. Darby had never stamped her foot in her life, but she was losing all power of reasoning.

"Well?"

"*Well.*" Darby reached out, grabbed the placard out of his hand and broke it across her knee.

He shifted his stance irritably. "Does that mean that you're going to be stubborn about this?"

She had never been angrier, but for one ridiculous moment she almost broke out laughing. He looked *so* goofy with that white beard, round belly, and those outrageous granny glasses perched on the tip of his cherry-red nose.

"I know a nice little Italian restaurant where we

can be alone," he coaxed softly. "Come on, Darby, give me a chance to show you that I'm not always the jerk you think I am."

Shaking her head, Darby turned and wordlessly walked off, leaving him standing with the broken placard at his feet.

"I suppose this means we're back to square one again?" he called after her.

She refused to answer.

"Yeah, Benderman," Cody muttered, leaning down to gather up his broken placard humbly. "That's what it means, all right."

By the time Darby reached the mall, she was calmer. Though Cody infuriated her as no other man had in her life, she had to admit that she was strongly drawn to him. So much so that he was beginning to terrify her. The *last* thing she needed was to fall in love, especially with someone like Cody Benderman. Falling in love meant commitment, and she wasn't ready to commit.

She had goals, goals she had worked too hard for just to toss them all aside in the name of love. A man like Cody Benderman would want children and a home and all the trappings she couldn't afford even to consider at this point in her life. No, no matter how strong her attraction for this man was becoming, she was going to ignore it.

The parking lot was full, so she was forced to

park on the very back row and tramp through puddles of slush to the stores. By the time she reached the mall entrance, her feet felt like two-hundred-pound blocks of ice.

Inside, shoppers were packed wall to wall. Even the recorded Christmas music seemed tired. The haggard old Santa who sat on a big chair in the center of the mall looked as if one too many children had cried into his now-bedraggled beard.

Darby knew that her run-in with Cody had dampened her already feeble Christmas spirit; she would have to struggle to get any shopping done at all.

By eight o'clock she sank down on a wooden bench to survey her rumpled shopping bag dismally. She had purchased one pair of gloves.

"Get a grip on yourself, Darb. At this rate you'll never get it finished."

An hour later she was beginning to feel better. Now she had six bags to maneuver through the crowd, but she'd at least finished most of her Christmas list. She'd even found some nice Christmas cards that would have to be mailed within the next week if she expected them to arrive before Christmas.

"Excuse me," Darby said, shouldering past a group of teenagers. "Pardon me."

Spotting the store she was going to next, she grimly forged her way down the mall. She wanted to purchase a silk nightgown with a matching robe for her mother, then she would go home and have a nervous breakdown.

The lingerie department was upstairs, so she had to maneuver the six bags up the escalator.

Thirty minutes later she had found the perfect night set, had paid for it, and had breathed a sigh of relief. Trying to combine a few of her purchases didn't work, so, balancing six bags and a large box, she eased her way onto the escalator again.

Her head ached, her feet hurt, and her hands hurt from hanging on to the bags and boxes, but the madness was over for another year.

However, if one more person stepped on her, bumped into her, or pushed her out of the way, she *was* going to scream.

Just as she was about to step off the escalator, she felt a heavy object strike the back of her heel. The heel snapped, and her ankle turned.

Stumbling off the escalator, Darby struggled to right herself. She balanced, her foot hanging off the broken shoe, shell-shocked.

Whirling, her eyes searched for the idiot who'd done this to her. Her mouth dropped open then snapped shut. She'd spotted the culprit.

Standing there with a red face and an apology was Cody.

"Now before you start accusing me of following you, I want you to know I wasn't. How was I to know you would be out here?" he asked defensively.

Darby glanced down at her shoe. The heel was gone. There was no way she could even pretend to keep it on until she got to the car.

Her heart sank. It was a perfectly awful ending to a perfectly awful day. Now she would have to walk barefoot in the snow, miles across the parking lot to her car. If she was lucky, she might only catch pneumonia and be in bed until January.

"Are you all right?"

"Oh, I'm just dandy. Just *dandy*," she snapped. "Why wouldn't I be? I'm exhausted, standing in the middle of the mall barefoot. It's snowing outside, and my car is parked four miles away. Life couldn't be sweeter."

She knew she was being obnoxious, but she just didn't care.

Before she knew what he was doing, Cody had leaned over and scooped her up, packages and all.

"Put me down!" she gasped.

Stone-faced, Cody gathered her more tightly into his arms and began to maneuver his way through the crowd.

"Cody, you are upsetting me again," she warned.

"So? What's new?"

"We're making a scene." Her face colored when she saw the stares of shoppers.

"You're making a scene," Cody reminded her. "Not me this time."

Shouldering the glass doors open, Cody strode out into the parking lot with her. Snow was falling heavily now, and the cold wind sent a rattle down Darby's spine.

"Where's your car?"

"Four miles down that way." Darby pointed to the east lot.

"Hell, forget it. Mine's closer."

Five minutes later he opened the passenger door of a black Bronco and perched Darby on the high seat.

"Give me the bags, and I'll put them in the back."

"No," she said stubbornly, trying to squirm off the seat, "I don't need your help."

"Look," Cody said, leaning in the door. His breath made frosty plumes in the cold air. "I stepped on your shoe and broke off the heel. The least I can do is drive you to your car."

Darby sighed, realizing that he was right. She couldn't walk to her car with only one shoe. "Oh, all right. I just want to go home."

Tucking her and the packages in the seat, Cody closed the door and walked around the Bronco to the driver's side.

Starting the engine, he glanced over at her. Her head was resting on the back of the seat and her eyes were fixed on the ceiling wearily.

"You look shot. Have you had dinner yet?"

"Thank you very much, and no, I haven't," Darby murmured, suddenly realizing how hungry she was.

Backing out of the parking space, he said quietly, "If you won't let me buy you spaghetti, then at least share a hamburger with me."

Darby was too exhausted to fight him anymore. "All right," she said, "but I'm buying."

Grinning, Cody wheeled out of the lot. "Have it your way."

They drove to a drive-in restaurant so that Darby wouldn't have to get out and gave their order to a waitress dressed as one of Santa's reindeer.

"Bet she's about to freeze her antlers off," Darby commented, eyeing the girl's preposterously short skirt.

"Oh, I don't know," Cody said, releasing his car seat so that he had more leg room. "I imagine if she tried hard enough, she'd find some animal lover willing to keep her warm."

Darby glanced at him and wrinkled her nose. "Men."

"You got something against them?"

"No."

He smiled. "Good."

Leaning back, she let the warm air from the heater drift over her. The small front seat was cozy and intimate. "I should have gone straight home after work instead of trying to shop."

"What do you do for the holidays? Do you have family here in Boston?"

"I go home—which is about twenty miles from

here. Mom still puts up a gigantic tree. And she always has her shopping done by the first of December while I'm always rushing around trying to finish on the twenty-fourth."

"You have brothers and sisters?"

"Two sisters. One's married to a banker, and the other is doomed to be an old maid. What about you? Have you always lived here?"

"All my life."

The waitress brought their hamburgers and hot chocolate.

They chatted amicably as they ate. The occasional silences between them were easier now, more comfortable.

Darby sipped the last of her hot chocolate as Cody glanced at her and smiled.

Remnants of whipped cream made a tempting white mustache under her nose. He leaned over and ran his finger along her upper lip lightly. "I don't suppose you'd let me kiss that off for you?"

She gazed up at him, realizing she couldn't keep the barrier between them much longer. He was making it impossible to keep him at a distance.

"Why do you say those kinds of things?"

His gazed deepened. "Why do you find it so offensive that I would want to kiss you?"

"I don't find it offensive . . . it's just . . . unsettling."

He took her cup from her hand and placed it

back on the tray. Darby felt briefly let down when it seemed he was willing to let the subject slide.

A short time later the Bronco drew up beside her car in the now almost deserted mall parking lot.

He insisted upon helping her out, and into her own car. "I'll follow you," he said as she started the BMW engine.

"It really isn't necessary," she protested.

"I have to go that way anyway. If I decide to turn off sooner I'll honk."

Suddenly feeling very shy, Darby extended her hand to him. "Thank you for the hamburger."

He took her hand and held it in his for a moment. "My pleasure."

When Darby pulled into her driveway thirty minutes later, the headlights of the Bronco turned in right behind her.

Before she could open the car door, Cody had opened it for her. Lifting her up into his arms, he carried her through the snow to the front door.

They were both laughing when he finally set her down, groaning about his aching back. Balancing on one foot, trying to hold the shoeless one off the wet porch, she leaned against him and unlocked the door.

She turned to say good night and discovered their faces were only inches away.

For a very long moment they didn't say anything. They simply looked at each other, trying to absorb the magnitude of what was happening.

Their breathing gradually slowed, then became shallow as his head lowered, his mouth brushing against hers lightly. "You're still going to object to me kissing you?" he said softly.

Darby nodded as their tongues tasted each other. She tasted cold and sweet, and he tasted warm and male. She couldn't remember ever wanting this much or needing like this. An ache began to build in her.

Holding her closer, Cody wanted to make her aware of how she affected him.

"Cody, please," she murmured.

"I'm not going to kiss you or touch you in any way—not until you want it as much as I do."

His mouth was so close, so agonizingly close now. Their breath was one in the cold night air as he moved against her, brutally assaulting her senses.

"Cody, please . . ."

"Please what?"

She sighed, tired of fighting it now. "Please kiss me."

Taking his time, he lowered his mouth, then began to close over hers hungrily. Warmed by her immediate response, he lifted her up into his arms and deepened the kiss and deepened and deepened it.

Darby was suddenly clinging to him, unaware that she'd reached out. Her body grew warm with desire, but he didn't stop. She had never met a man who touched every fiber of her soul and left her aching for more.

When their lips finally parted, they were both breathing heavily.

"I want to see you again," he said softly.

"No—"

"Forget the business crap. I'll take down the display if that's what it takes."

"No . . . I don't want you to do that." Darby realized she *didn't* want him to do that—not because of her. It wouldn't be right. He loved children, and she knew in her heart that he wasn't intentionally creating a public nuisance. Somehow, she would work that part of the problem out. But what would she do about her own problem of falling in love with him?

His features grew serious as he gazed down on her. "You say the word, lady. If you won't mix business with pleasure, then one or the other is going to have to go."

"Cody, you don't understand. It isn't just business. I'm just not ready for this yet—"

"For what?" he interrupted. "Don't tell me you don't feel what's happening between us." He held her even closer, taking her breath with his boldness. "It's *never* happened to me this fast or this forcefully," he whispered huskily.

"Nor to me," she whispered back, "but I know in my heart that you would want more—much more than I'm capable of giving right now."

"Such as?"

"Such as marriage and children." She knew without being told that Cody Benderman was ready to put down roots. He wasn't exactly a kid anymore, nor was she. But she didn't feel at this point in her life that she could successfully juggle a career and marriage and do either one of them justice.

Disappointment filtered through Cody's features now. "You don't want marriage and children?"

"Not yet—not for years. I have my career—"

"You can have your career. Hundreds of women balance a career and a family every day," he argued.

"But I'm not capable of balancing both—at least not yet."

Panic seized her. What was she *doing* standing here arguing about marriage with a man she hadn't even gone on an official date with yet!

Cody knew when to push, and when not to. Letting his hands drop to his sides, he smiled. "Hey, all right. Let's not get emotional about this. It was just a simple kiss, not a marriage proposal."

Squeezing her shoulder, he kissed her forehead platonically. "You better get to bed. It's late."

Stunned, Darby watched as he walked down

the steps and disappeared around the side of the house.

A moment later she heard the Bronco start, and she watched as he backed out of the drive and drove off.

A simple kiss? she thought frantically. Every cell in her ached from his "simple" kiss.

She was really panicked now. She didn't find the kiss simple and she seriously doubted that Cody had meant it to be.

And she was beginning to realize that nothing about Cody Benderman was simple.

•

Six

"Has the jury reached its verdict?"

"We have, Your Honor." The bailiff walked over and accepted the verdict, then turned and approached the bench. He handed the slip of paper to Judge Moorhouse.

After looking at the verdict, Judge Moorhouse laid the paper aside. "Would the defendant please rise?"

Darby stood with her client.

"The jury finds for the plaintiff. Defendant is ordered to pay all damages as outlined in the original complaint plus all court costs resulting from this action."

Judge Moorhouse picked up his gavel and rapped it firmly. "Court dismissed."

Turning to her client, Darby put her hand on Burke Wedlock's shoulder. "I'm sorry, Burke. We just didn't have a strong enough case."

"Oh, I know," Burke admitted, "I'm guilty as hell. I just wasn't about to let Bud Matthison get off without a fight."

Burke strolled out of the courtroom a happy man.

Sinking back down onto her chair, Darby wondered why she hadn't just gone to beauty school instead of law school.

It was after eight that evening when Darby reached her development. She was coming down with a miserable cold and longed for a hot bath and complete solitude.

In addition to her disappointment with Burke Wedlock in court this afternoon, Cody Benderman was plaguing her thoughts. His kiss the night before still hummed through her veins. She had to wonder how she could have let herself become so distracted by a man she barely knew. And yet she was. Almost to the point of preoccupation. For the first time in her career she realized that she was no longer able to remain emotionally detached from a case.

Each time she worked on her defense of *Haven Heights* v. *Benderman*, Cody's face popped into her mind. Not Cordell Benderman, but Cody Benderman, the man who was nothing but a kid at heart. She could hear the sounds of children's laughter as Cody, in a Santa suit, handed out candy canes to little tots. Images assailed her: the warm glow of a nativity scene, the harmonious strains of "Silent Night" made even more exquisite by the sight of the Christ Child wrapped in swaddling clothes and lying in a manger—a manger Cody had told her he had spent long nights building in his cold garage; Snow White skating with her prince as snow fell softly—Cody, laughing as he had carried her in his arms across the mall parking lot . . .

Stop it, Darby berated herself irritably. If she kept this up, she would be forced to hand the case over to Victor, and Cody would end up losing.

Now she wasn't making sense. She was the Kinnitses' lawyer, not Cody Benderman's!

Wheeling into the cul-de-sac, her foot hit the pedal, locking the brakes. Two gravel trucks, a backhoe, and that blasted dozer were parked squarely in her way.

She seethed, knowing that Cody was playing games again. She eyed the pile of gravel blocking her driveway. It was the size of the Empire State Building. Well, she wasn't in any mood for any more games. Not with Cody Benderman.

Easing the BMW right in front of the pile of gravel, she got out and left it. Let him put *that* in his pipe and smoke it, she muttered.

After a hot bath and two industrial-strength cold pills, she slipped into her worn robe and fuzzy slippers, then sat down on the side of her bed to open her mail. Atop the pile was a notice from the city reminding her that she had only eight weeks to assign a contractor to install the sewer line running from her house to the street and to arrange for hookup.

"Wonderful." She tossed the letter straight up into the air. "Now my yard will be completely mutilated."

Glancing at the phone, she thought about calling Cody. She didn't have the slightest idea why, but all of a sudden she just wanted to hear his voice. Was she losing her mind? Probably. It must be the flu.

Lying down on the bed, she gathered her pillow and held it tightly against her breasts, forcing herself to remember her goals and how important it was for her to accomplish them. She had worked hard to get where she was. She couldn't allow an arrogant, curly-headed, damnably good-looking construction worker, who happened to have the most beautiful blue eyes in the entire world, to spoil it for her.

She just couldn't.

*   *   *

At seven the next morning, Darby emerged from the shower. Someone was pounding on her front door.

She grabbed her robe and whipped it on. Cinching the belt around her waist, she hurriedly padded down the hallway to answer the door. She guessed that it would be Cody wanting to know what her car was doing parked in *his* way.

She yanked the door open. Her handsome nemesis leaned insolently against the doorframe.

Her pulse went into a gallop, the way it always did now when she was confronted with his brawny, outdoorsy good looks.

"Hello, Benderman."

His forefinger touched the brim of his hard hat respectfully. "Morning, counselor."

His blue eyes surveyed her lackadaisically, but Darby didn't mind. She even found herself wondering what it would be like to lie in bed with him early in the morning and give that same impudent gaze permission to roam with leisure. Her pulse began to beat even more erratically.

"Your car's in front of my chat pile. You trying to get my attention?" he asked.

Leaning against the opposite side of the doorframe, she met his gaze straightforwardly. "No. Do I have to try?"

His eyes skimmed the damp robe that was

nicely molded to her small breasts. "Your car's in my way, Ms. Piper."

She gazed back at him, her eyes admiring his lean frame, his broad shoulders, his curly hair, his tan—which she was sure meant a recent vacation to Florida—and his eyes . . . she loved those bedroom eyes. "Correction: Your rock pile is in my way, Mr. Benderman."

"Correction: I put it there purposely."

She shook her head. "Dare I ask why?"

"Because annoying you seems to be the only way I can get your attention."

"If you want my attention, then please stop hitting me in the checkbook. You see, Mr. Benderman, I'm not skilled at maneuvering chat piles, and I really can't afford another towing bill. I have to save my money to hook up to the new sewer lines."

He shrugged. "Marry me, and I'll see that you're connected free of charge."

She dropped her hands in surprise. Her robe opened slightly, allowing the fabric to gap—ever, ever so discreetly. She saw how the innocent slip made his eyes darken and took impudent delight in it.

"Your offer was thoughtful, but I really couldn't," she said.

Shame on you, Darby. You've never acted this way with a man before.

"You're sure?"

"I'm sure."

He noticed that the front of her robe gapped just a *tiny* bit more, revealing the soft, inviting swells. "Then why don't we have breakfast together?" He asked. "That isn't such a big commitment."

"Sorry, can't do that either."

His gaze rested on the tempting display of flesh, but his manner remained unruffled. "You play hard to get, don't you?"

She nodded. "Sorry, you're not in my long-range goal."

"Any man? Or just me in particular?"

"You, in particular."

He grinned, a lazy, self-assured grin that made her wonder who was playing with whom.

"Well, I will be." Leaning forward, Cody casually drew the front of her robe back together.

Stepping backward, she stared at him, momentarily disarmed by the action.

He winked. "Wind's a little sharp. Wouldn't want you catching a chill."

Turning, he started off the porch. "You've got ten minutes to get your BMW out of the way, or I'll have it towed," he called over his shoulder.

Wincing, he grinned as he heard the door slam shut behind him.

* * *

Nine minutes later Darby bounded out of the front door, still half-dressed. The last thing she needed was another towing bill. Her teeth rattling against the cold, she dashed out to move the BMW.

The lock on the door was frozen solid. As the key jiggled in her shivering fingers, she realized she was risking pneumonia. Her cold had been worse this morning, and running out of the house without a coat wasn't too smart.

Cody spotted her struggling with the door and turned from the two men he had been speaking with. Striding across the street, he called to her, "What's wrong now?"

"The lock's frozen."

"What in the hell are you doing out here without a coat on?" he snapped.

"I was down to *one crummy* minute. I didn't have time to put a coat on," she snapped back.

He peeled out of his heavy jacket and draped it around her shoulders. The enveloping scent of his musky after-shave caused a swift reaction somewhere deep within her. "Get back inside the house. I'll move the car for you," he ordered.

"I am capable of moving my own car." Darby felt her eyes growing moist and a new round of sneezes coming on as she fumbled in her pocket for a tissue.

"Damn, are you going to *cry* about this?" he accused, stunned to think she'd fold so easily.

"I'm not crying! I have a cold—a miserable cold." She felt rotten. All she wanted to do was go back into the house, crawl into bed, and sleep until Christmas.

She jammed the key into the lock and forcefully jerked open the car door. Sliding behind the wheel, she started the engine, then threw the car into reverse. The car shot backward, narrowly missing the trench, the pile of gravel, and the dozer, and sending Cody scrambling for safety.

"You want me to bring you some chicken soup for that cold?" she heard him shout.

"No!"

"No, what?"

"No, thank you!"

Glancing into the rearview mirror, she saw that he was grinning at her.

She muttered something under her breath.

Chicken soup was the least of her problems.

Darby dragged into her office a little before nine. Today, *her* nose was cherry red.

After pouring herself a cup of coffee, she closed the door of her office and began phoning contractors for estimates on installing the connecting sewer lines from her house to the street.

The first two were booked into February, and the third didn't think the weather was going to cooperate well enough for them to take on any more work.

The fourth put her on hold for five minutes. As she was about to hang up, a man's voice came back on the line.

"Your condo gotta basement, sweetheart?"

When Darby said that it did, he groaned dramatically. "You know what that means," he said.

"No, I don't know what that means." But Darby had a sinking feeling she wasn't going to like his next revelation.

"It means it won't be a simple job."

"Of course not" she sighed. "Just how 'unsimple' is it?"

"Well, now, let's see. You're out there in the Gildersleeve Addition"—she could hear him scribbling—"and there'll be extra plumbing to come out of the basement, depending upon where the main-line hookup is. Then there's the lift pump. Then there'll be the cost of running the line across the yard, the pipe, and the chat, and the hookup to the street." The continuous hum of the adding machine came across the phone line.

Darby closed her eyes sickly.

The figure he finally gave her made her head spin. "Well, thank you . . . I'll take this under consideration."

Dropping the receiver back into its cradle, she leaned back on her chair, feeling drained.

A few moments later she left her office, carrying

her briefcase. "Gail, I've had it. This cold has got me down. I'm going home for the day."

Waving goodbye, Gail went on busily forwarding calls. "You coming in tomorrow?"

"I have to be in court at ten."

"Hope you can make it, Rudolph!"

Arriving home, Darby found a note tacked on her door. Bracing herself, she opened the folded piece of paper. It was from the gas company. The construction crew had hit a main gas line. Everyone on the street would have to arrange to have their furnace and pilot lights relit. Darby groaned. That meant that the hot-water heater had been off too. No hot bath.

She built a fire in the fireplace, then crawled into bed, assuring herself that everything had gone wrong that could go wrong. If she could just sleep for a few blissful hours, she could cope.

While she was sleeping, the electricity went off. Darby slept straight through. When she finally awoke, she sat up, dazed, trying to focus on the clock. She frowned. Three? *Three* A.M.? *It can't be three* A.M. *It's light outside!*

Scrambling out of bed, she checked her quartz watch. It was *nine* A.M. She was due in court at *ten!* She bolted for the bathroom, took a brisk shower, dressed in the first thing she could find, and ran headlong out to her car.

Cody was about to climb aboard a dozer when he saw her dart out of the house. Relieved to see her, he called out, "Hey! Where were you last night?"

"In bed!"

"With whom?"

"Very funny!"

"I called you *three* times, and you weren't home!"

After starting her car, Darby backed out of her driveway. Pausing beside the dozer, she hurriedly rolled down her window. "I didn't hear the phone. I'd taken so many cold pills that I've been out for the past few hours."

Leaning his arm on the window, he studied her with a concerned gaze. "You okay?"

"I'm fine." It occurred to her that it was nice, really nice, to have someone concerned about her.

"You ready to marry me yet?"

She sighed, shaking her head at him. How was she supposed to take such an outrageous statement? "Are you asking seriously this time?"

A smile touched the corners of his mouth. "Would you seriously consider it?" he countered.

She rolled her eyes. This man was one of a kind. "Don't you think it would be appropriate if we had at least one date before we contemplated such a momentous decision?"

He shrugged. "I've been trying to get you to go out with me for days."

Glancing at her watch, she saw that she was hopelessly late. "Darn, late again."

"Gee, Darby, you really should do something about that," he said seriously. "You're going to make some judge mad one of these days, always showing up late."

He jumped back as spray of gravel from the car's tires flew at him.

Darby rushed in the courtroom just as the clerk was calling her case. It wasn't until lunch that she realized she had a big run in her hose and still had her boots on.

Over a toasted cheese sandwich and coffee, she thought about Cody Benderman and what he'd brought into her life.

He'd brought chaos. Complete chaos. Yet she was beginning to welcome the excitement that he'd introduced into her previously dull routine. Since they'd met, she'd felt happier, more alive.

The progression of her thoughts began to frighten her. Could she be falling in love with Cordell Benderman? The concept seemed ludicrous, but how many times could a stranger propose to her without prompting her to wonder what type of man it was that she'd *really* consider spending her life with.

Darby was beginning to understand that Cody was the type of man she could easily spend her life with. And that made him even more of a threat to the future she'd planned.

She had to come to grips with her feelings—and thwart them. From now on, she would just go out of her way to avoid bumping into him. Once the suit was over and the construction work in her area completed, she would forget all about Cody Benderman.

It should be very simple.

"Hi," said Darby wearily after she'd answered her doorbell around nine that evening.

"Hi," Cody returned. "Want me to light your fire?"

"I don't think so," she replied coolly.

"Your pilot light? Gas has been out again today."

Sighing, Darby stepped aside and let Cody enter her condo. Her eyes surveyed the expensive leather jacket and Italian loafers he was wearing. The man looked good, she had to give him that.

Striding across the room, Cody's eyes took in the tasteful furnishing. "Nice."

"Thanks."

"I assume the furnace is downstairs?" He glanced at her, his eyes skimming her bare legs and the short, silk robe she was wearing.

"Yes."

Darby trailed behind him as they walked down the dimly lit stairway to the basement. "Don't you ever go home?"

"Occasionally. I just thought with the utility crew backed up the way it is, you might need my help. How's the cold?"

"Better. . . . Can't you guys ever dig without hitting a gas line?" she asked. "I had to take another cold shower tonight."

"My heart bleeds for you," he said. Lying down on his back, he removed the door from the hot-water heater. "I've taken my fair share of cold showers."

Leaning against the washing machine, she noted the irony in his voice and grinned. "I'll bet you have."

After a moment he had the heater lit and had moved on to the furnace.

She watched him for a moment, and then parried lightly, "Say, does your marriage proposal still hold?"

He glanced up.

She shrugged, realizing she was flirting. "I called the plumbing contractors yesterday. I've decided it would be cheaper to marry you."

He turned his attention back to the furnace pilot light. "Well, I'm free tomorrow afternoon if you are."

"Tomorrow afternoon?" She pretended to consider it.

"We could leave around three and have that first date if that's still worrying you." Blowing out the match, he rose to stand. "Then we could fly to Vegas and get married."

For the first time Darby noticed how tired he looked. She knew that he had to be putting in long days. He was on the job hours before she went to work and still busy when she got home.

"You look tired," she said softly.

"I am."

"Have you eaten?"

"Not since around noon."

Sighing, she took his arm and began to walk him to the stairway. "I don't have much in the refrigerator, but I think I can manage eggs and toast."

"Breakfast?" He wrinkled his nose.

"You don't like breakfast?"

"Not for dinner. How about pizza?"

"I'm too far out for delivery."

"No kidding? Lucky I picked up one on my way over."

She eyed him sourly as they climbed the stairs together. "How did you know that I would even be home?"

"I didn't—but there's no law against hoping, is there?"

"More wine?"

Cody held up his glass, and Darby filled it. Stepping over him, she seated herself beside him on the rug in front of the fireplace.

Outside the wind whistled under the eaves, but inside it was warm and cozy. Contented, she rested her head against a cushion of the sofa and she stared at the flames. "By the way, I hate pepperoni."

"Lord, I'd hate to feed you something you liked," he said. "You ate four pieces."

"Only to be nice."

Leaning over, he lightly brushed his mouth across hers. A hot, sweet ache began somewhere in the pit of her stomach as Darby moved closer. They exchanged a brief, kiss, neither permissive nor discouraging.

His hand slipped to her bare leg, gently massaging her soft skin. "Good, I like it when you're trying to be nice to me."

It wasn't his tone, but rather the look in his eyes that told Darby she would be wise to retreat. She cleared her throat and asked, "Why aren't you home tending your display?"

"Too much traffic and confusion." He leaned to kiss her again as she tried to scoot away.

"Who's handing out candy canes to all the bad little girls?"

Cody leaned back, letting her go momentarily. Smiling, he gazed at her. "I was surprised to see you there that night."

"I was surprised when Santa refused to give me my candy."

He shrugged, extending his hand to her. "You can have anything of Santa's you want."

Sobering, Darby looked back at him. "Cody, please . . ."

Letting his hand drop back to his side, he picked up his glass. "I don't know why you're so frightened."

"I don't either . . . but I am," she confessed.

"There must be a reason." he prodded.

"Well, maybe it's because I want everything else in order before I . . ."

"Fall in love?"

"Yes. I'm not a superwoman. It isn't a matter of being a feminist. I want a home and family of my own, but I also want to be able to give my husband and my children the attention they deserve. It's usually the children who suffer when the demands of the mother's job require her total attention. In another few years I'll have the partnership, and a sound practice. I'll be able to go to PTA meetings and circuses and come home and still be the kind of wife to my husband that I want to be. But right now, I don't feel I can do that. Do you understand?"

"I understand." He lifted his glass in a conciliatory salute. "So, what were you going to do tonight before I interrupted?"

"Address Christmas cards."

"Have any extras?"

Tilting her head, she smiled at him. "How many do you need?"

"Just three or four."

Darby stepped over him again, reaching for the box of cards lying on the end table. "Good, I have around thirty to address. You can help."

Cody viewed the pair of bare, shapely legs straddling him and groaned. "Great."

For the next couple of hours they worked addressing holiday cards to Darby's business associates.

Around one FurBall, Darby's Persian cat, wandered through.

The large cat moseyed over to Cody, walked across his lap, then ambled on to the sofa.

Cody's eyes immediately began to water.

Darby looked at him in surprise. "You aren't allergic to cats, are you?"

As he rubbed his eyes with his fists, she realized that he was. "Not too bad," he lied.

She stood, picked up her cat, and hurriedly carried him out of the room.

"You don't need to do that," he called, then she heard him sneeze four times in a row.

"Sorry, FurBall," she said softly. "We have a small problem."

Cody had started on her personal card list when Darby came back in the room.

He looked up accusingly. "Who's 'Jeff'?"

"Just a man I know."

A moment later he sealed the envelope and reached for another one. Scanning the list, he began writing again. "Who's 'Jacques'?"

"Just a man I know."

Nonchalantly, he selected a few cards from the pile and began addressing them.

Darby glanced over, frowning when she read the name on the envelope. "Who's 'Jody'?"

"Just a girl I know," he said absently. He tossed the envelope aside and reached for another card.

"Who's 'Sharon'?" she asked a few minutes later, not quite as cordially as she had before.

"Just a girl—"

"—you know," she finished.

"Right." He ducked as the box of cards came flying in his direction.

A moment later they tumbled onto the rug, playfully wrestling with each other. When Cody discovered that she was ticklish, she was soon left begging for mercy.

When he finally allowed her time to catch her breath, she lay on top of him, resting her cheek on his.

As he closed his eyes Cody slipped his hands up to hold her closer. "Let me just hold you," he whispered quietly. "I've wanted to from the first day I saw you."

Lifting her head, she gazed into his eyes.

"Please . . . don't say that . . . it scares me
so. . . ."

"It shouldn't." He suddenly pulled her against
him. "Give us a chance, Darby. I won't stand in
the way of your goals." His mouth searched for
hers hungrily.

She didn't want it to happen.

It was the last thing in the world he had
planned on happening.

Darby felt his hands parting her robe, then his
hands sliding beneath her gown, his palms warm
and searching against her bare flesh.

She started to murmur her protests, but her
body caught fire. Suddenly, both his and her
hands were everywhere, searching, touching,
pressing, stroking.

"Oh, Lord," she whispered, burying her fingers
in the thick, brown mass of curls that grew at
the nape of his neck. She could feel her blood
begin to pound as his hands became bolder and
surer.

She clung to him, praying that he would stop
and praying that he wouldn't.

His fingers fumbled with her gown, parting it,
then slipping it off her shoulders. She felt the
fabric give, then slip away. His mouth was at her
ear, huskily whispering her name as his hand
slid down her naked length.

He rolled her beneath him, and she found herself pressed against him willingly. Their mouths

fused together hotly as he struggled out of his clothes. As he cast them aside with impatience his lips left hers for an instant.

Then he came back to her, searching, seeking, imploring.

The rug felt rough against her back as warm, hard flesh met hers. Whispering his love, he took her, his eyes assuring her that it was more than need that drove him.

Never before had it been so fast, so furious, or so unrestrained for either of them.

The world suddenly was wrapped in clouds of silk-soft mists. Swept away by a firestorm of passion, Darby was no longer able to deny what Cody had been saying all along. They were meant for each other as surely as the moon and the stars.

Love and passion clouded her mind, and she no longer tried to separate them as she gave her whole being—her very soul—to the man she held in her arms.

When the storm was over, they lay quiet against one another, shaken.

"Oh, Darb . . . I meant for this to happen in a more romantic place," he whispered, cradling her head against his chest.

Stunned, Darby allowed him to hold her. She couldn't find the words to tell him what was in her heart. The words frightened her too much.

"What are you thinking?" he whispered. "Talk to me, sweetheart."

She lifted her head and blurted out "I'm thinking this shouldn't have happened."

He saw the horrified look on her face. Hurt clouded his eyes, but he accepted her words calmly. A moment later he rose and quietly began to dress.

Moments later she stiffened as she heard her front door close.

Sinking back down to the sofa, she sat stunned, realizing that this time it was unlikely he would ever be back.

Seven

"There must be some way to reach a compromise on this," Darby muttered as she paced back and forth in front of Carter's desk the next morning. She was tense and on edge. From the dark circles under her eyes, it was obvious that she hadn't slept well the night before.

She paused in her tracks and murmured, "There must be a way to satisfy the Kinnitses and their neighbors without interfering with Cody's good-hearted intentions."

Carter's brows lifted oddly. " 'Good-hearted intentions'? What's happened to the insensitive jerk who should be run out of town on a rail?"

She paused, realizing how odd this change in her attitude must seem. She was defending the defendant instead of trying to hang him. "I know it sounds like I'm being disloyal, but I just don't think it's right that Cody has to take down his Christmas decorations . . . he doesn't mean any harm. . . ." As her voice trailed off, she began pacing again.

"My, my." Carter leaned back in his chair, watching her pace. "What brought this on?"

"Nothing—it just isn't right that when a man tries to bring a little happiness into the world, he should have to go to court and defend his actions. It isn't fair."

"Sometimes right isn't fair."

"But it should be," she argued. "At least in this case it should be. And if I were worth my salt, I'd be able to find a way to make it both right *and* fair . . . for everyone concerned."

"Darby, you're an outstanding attorney. You do a superb job defending your clients' rights. But you must bear in mind the Kinnitses are your clients, not Benderman."

She stopped pacing and slumped into a chair, drained. "You're right. I'm not doing my job."

"I didn't say that."

"You don't have to. We both know it. I'm the attorney for the plaintiff. I shouldn't be worrying about what Cody is going to do with his yard decorations once I beat his tail off in court."

Carter chuckled softly, but concern seeped into his voice now. "Cody? You're not becoming personally involved with Cordell Benderman, are you?"

"Personally involved?" She almost laughed out loud. Yes, she supposed that she could say she was becoming "personally involved" with Cody.

"No," she replied, knowing it was a bold-faced lie. "That wouldn't be ethical."

"That wasn't my question. Are you becoming personally involved with him?"

"Well . . . it would be awfully easy to be," she said

"Darby." Carter's tone was sterner now.

She sighed, realizing that she had lost all perspective. "I know . . . but he's not an easy man to dislike. He has all the right ingredients. He's confident almost to the point of being arrogant, yet he isn't arrogant. He just knows what he wants and goes after it. He has a great sense of humor, and a sense of the outrageous. But he's also charming, sensitive, witty, and caring. When I ruined my stockings and shoes wading out to his dozer, he sent two dozen red roses and three pair of silk stockings. And if you've seen that display in his yard—"

"I have," Carter admitted sheepishly. "Took the grandkids by a couple of nights ago. Santa gave them each a candy cane."

Darby edged forward in her chair, the sparkle returning to her eyes. "Santa is Cody, when Cody has the time to be."

"My, my." Carter smiled, realizing that he had never seen Darby so animated, so vitally alive. Falling in love was becoming on her. "So," he said softly, "what do you intend to do about this wonderful man?"

She shook her head wistfully. "I honestly don't know."

"Well, maybe you should give the matter serious thought. If Benderman's that good, you wouldn't want to let him slip through your fingers."

Darby glanced up, surprised. Carter had never made any comments on the men she'd dated. "You old fraud," she accused. "You'd like me to become 'personally involved' with Cody, wouldn't you?"

"I just want you to be happy."

"Oh, Carter." Her gaze grew affectionate now. "Cody does make me happy, but he's come into my life at the wrong time. I still have things I want to do before I get caught up in a relationship that I would want to make permanent."

"Well, love doesn't always arrive at the most convenient time," he admitted. "And it doesn't always go away when we want it to."

"I know. That's what's worrying me."

"But I do have a more positive thought concerning the impasse in the case. Have you considered contacting the city about designating a small park in the downtown area for the display? Perhaps Benderman would consider donating his decorations to the park, in exchange for their promise to put up the display each season?"

Darby's face sobered. "No . . . the thought hadn't entered my mind."

"Could it possibly be that you're too close to the case?" Carter suggested, discreetly.

She rose to her feet and began to pace more purposefully. Her mind whirled with new possibilities. "Of course . . . it would be the perfect solution. Cody could donate the decorations to the city, and they could display the scenes year after year. If we could find a park with adequate parking, the city could even bring in extra revenue from it." She paced faster, falling in love with the idea. "Cody could go down to the park every night if he wanted and watch the children—it wouldn't be as if it weren't his, it would just be relocated— oh, Carter!" She turned, her face radiant with relief. "It's perfect. Absolutely perfect!"

"Good, but I caution you, the city may not share your enthusiasm."

"Oh, they have to," she said. She refused to consider any negative thoughts. All of a sudden she was brimming with the Christmas spirit. "It's Christmas, Carter," she reminded him, leaning over to squeeze his shoulder. "Christmas!"

Darby spent the entire afternoon talking to City Hall. By four she felt she was making some headway. The powers that be were finally persuaded to put the matter on the City Council agenda for the next meeting.

Hanging up the phone, she sighed, swiveled around in her chair, and stared out the window happily. Once the agenda item was agreed upon, she would call Jeff and offer the compromise. She felt sure that all parties involved in the suit would be delighted to have a case end without having to go to court.

Her exhilaration began to turn to something quite different when she thought about Cody. A delicious tingle worked its way through her as she thought about the way he had made love to her the night before.

It had happened so fast, so frenzied. And it had been so perfectly, perfect. Until she'd made him leave.

She sat for a long time, her head resting against the back of her chair, her eyes closed. She could hear the muted sounds of her colleagues leaving the office, calling their good nights to Gail. Christmas carols floated softly beneath her closed doors, and outside her window lights began to go on in the Marketplace, twinkling merrily in the growing dusk.

She tried very hard to sort through her feelings. What she wanted and what she needed suddenly became very hard to separate. She hadn't wanted new sewer lines, but she had them. She hadn't wanted to fall for Cody Benderman, but she had. She didn't want to *be* in love, but she was. She didn't want to jeopardize her future, but she knew in her heart that she was about to.

Her eyes opened slowly, her gaze fastening on the phone.

She believed that she would just call him and tell him she loved him.

A moment later she believed that she wouldn't.

It was close to seven before she opened her eyes again. It was dark outside. She still had the long drive home, and FurBall was out of cat food again.

She bundled up, pulled on her galoshes, and trudged out of the office. After riding the empty elevator down fifteen floors, she headed for the parking garage.

The supermarket wasn't crowded, and she finished her shopping quickly. She carried her bags out to her car. She juggled the sacks, trying to unlock the trunk.

As she bent over, she suddenly felt something solid smack her backside. Turning around, she saw the residue of a snowball peeling away from her coat.

Scowling, she looked to see who'd thrown it.

Cody was leaning against his Bronco, grinning.

Her heart raced in spite of herself. Here he was

again, and she couldn't have been happier to see him. She now knew why she'd been so frightened all day. She had been terrified that she wouldn't see him again outside a courtroom.

"Are you following me?" she asked, trying not to smile.

"Yes, ma'am, but you're getting hard to keep up with."

Unable to resist the temptation, Darby scooped up a handful of snow and quickly formed it into a solid ball. With an aim honed by years of fighting with her sisters, she flung the warhead with deadly accuracy. Cody slid on the ice as he scrambled for cover.

"Hey!"

"Turnabout's fair play," she called back, ducking as he aimed another missile at her.

She straightened, heaving another one at him.

"Ha! Missed me!"

"You shouldn't start something you can't finish," she challenged.

"I always finish what I start." He sent another ball hurtling at her, which smacked the side of her head.

"Ha!" she returned, aiming another one at him.

Ducking the sudden onslaught of snowballs, Cody cowered behind the fender of his Bronco, systematically building an awesome arsenal.

When her meager supply was depleted, he calmly stepped out and let her have it.

A spirited snowball fight ensued, one that had supermarket customers smiling with amusement and hurriedly scrambling out of the danger zone.

Snowballs flew fast and furious, some reaching their targets but others hitting their cars. Most of Cody's second volley of snowballs splattered against Darby's car, sending a generous amount of snow down her collar. Finally, she took off her scarf and waved it as a white flag of surrender.

"Giving up?"

"No, I'm running out of ammunition, and I'm too cold to make more," Darby called back.

"Truce?"

"Truce." She stood, laughingly brushing the snow off her coat.

Cody strode across the snow-packed parking lot to meet her.

"You're pretty good."

"School champ," she said, dusting off her gloves. "Everyone always wanted to have me on their side at recess."

"I can understand that," he said softly. "I wouldn't mind having you on mine."

Her insides turned jittery again. She was tempted to tell him about how she'd spent her afternoon thinking about him—and about the idea for the display—but decided she wouldn't until she knew the city would agree.

"Want to?"

"What?" She'd been so caught up in her thoughts she hadn't been listening.

"Go sledding. I was by Rudman's Hill this afternoon. It looked like it was in perfect condition."

"I haven't been sledding in years." She smiled with delight.

"You haven't been sledding at all until you've gone with me," he corrected.

"I don't have a sled."

"I don't either, but we can get a couple inside."

She hesitated, but only for a moment. Why not? It would be fun. The heck with prudence.

"Okay, but I'll have to go home and feed FurBall first."

"Fine. We'll leave your car and take the Bronco. Let's go get the sleds." They fell into step and started back into the store.

"Dibs on the red one," Darby said, recalling the display at the front of the store. "I always had a red one when I was little."

"All right, you get the red one," Cody said. "Although red happens to be my favorite color."

"If you're very good, you can ride on mine."

He glanced down at her, the innuendo in his eyes bringing a blush to her already rosy cheeks. "I'm always very good. And don't you forget it."

They bought the sleds and Cody followed Darby home. While he waited, she fed FurBall and quickly changed into ski pants and a parka. Stamping on her boots, she joined Cody in the living room.

"Ready?"

"Ready."

They drove to Rudman's Hill. The hill was at the edge of a large housing development, and it was wide, offering a variety of slopes. Darby was disappointed to see that there were already a number of people there. She realized that she had been hoping that they'd be alone.

The night was crisp and cold. Stars twinkled in the velvety black sky. The moon bathed the hill with light as the sounds of laughter and squeals of delight rang out from children and adults alike.

Darby stood at the top of the hill watching two children careening downhill, one behind the other on a long sled.

"It's so beautiful," she said. Cody stood behind her on the hilltop, watching the fun. Drawing her close to him, he fitted their bodies together like spoons. He lowered his head and began kissing from her ear down the column of her neck.

Murmuring a halfhearted protest, she snuggled closer, drinking in the familiar scent of his soap and after-shave.

"I've thought about you all day," he whispered.

"And I've thought about you."

"Good." His tongue touched the lobe of her ear, and she snuggled against him even closer. "You smell good, counselor"—his tongue touched here and there—"and you taste good—"

They jumped back as three boys carrying a sled pushed and darted between them.

Smiling, Darby held out her hand to Cody. "Race you to the bottom."

"You're on!" He picked up his sled. "I'll be there to catch you when you arrive."

"Ha!"

He was already pushing off as she was climbing aboard her sled. She almost caught him, but he won.

Before long, another challenge was issued and met. Their breath was icy and clouded in the cold air. Ice crystals clung to their parkas and gloves. They wore a path down the hill that was so slick and fast that they had to cling to one another as they trudged back up again.

When they reached the top of the hill the last time, Darby collapsed in a heap on her sled. "I'm dead," she said dramatically.

Cody sat on his sled, grinning at her. "You're beautiful."

She rolled to her side, meeting his gaze. "You make me feel beautiful."

"You make me feel . . . everything. That's why I love you."

"Cody," she said softly. "Don't. . . ."

"Marry me, Darby," he coaxed gently. "Let's

make it a perfect Christmas. We can be married on Christmas Eve."

"No—but you can come home with me and I'll fix you some hot chocolate. I think the cold has addled your brain." She stood, dusting the snow off her parka.

"I'd rather have you," he said as they loaded the sleds into the car.

And I you, she thought, realizing that she was beginning to mean it.

They listened to Christmas carols on the radio as he drove back to the condo. Darby rested her head on his shoulder, his arm holding her close. The ache was building inside her, the nagging, sweet ache that devoured her when he was near. Now that she had tasted the forbidden fruit, would she be able to turn him away? The thought nagged at her.

Cody pulled into her driveway and switched off the motor, then turned to her. In the moonlight streaming through the car windows they gazed at each other silently.

It was as if she had spoken her troubled thoughts aloud, and he had heard.

"Does that offer of hot chocolate still stand?"

"Sure. With two marshmallows."

"You don't know how happy that makes me."

"Yes, I do, because it makes me happy," she admitted.

After shedding their parkas, gloves, and boots,

they went into the kitchen. Darby started the hot chocolate while Cody opened the bag of marshmallows. He popped one into his mouth and then turned to pop one into hers.

He grinned when she almost choked.

There was a white streak across his bottom lip, and before she thought, Darby reached up and brushed it off with her thumb.

Cody caught her wrist and licked her finger, his eyes never leaving hers.

Her breathing slowed as he pulled her closer and leaned over to brush her lips with his. His face was icy cold, but his lips were warm and they tasted of vanilla cream.

Murmuring her name, he drew her into his arms, and she went willingly.

"No," she breathed a moment later. "No." She pushed out of his arms, drawing a deep breath. She could not let him make love to her again. This time there could be no turning back, she knew.

His hands dropped back to his sides. "Damn, Darb, I'm getting tired of fighting you on this." He reached out and drew her into his arms again, not understanding, but not yet ready to give up on her.

She rested her head against his chest. There was so much confusion inside her. She did want him. So very, very much. But she wanted the future she'd planned too.

"All right, maybe we should forget the chocolate," he said quietly. "I've been pushing too hard." He gave her an understanding smile. "I'll give you a call later in the week."

She nodded, closing her eyes.

He turned and walked out of the kitchen.

Closing her eyes again, Darby leaned against the cabinet. She was doing the right thing, wasn't she? But if she were, then why was there this awful ache inside her? She heard the front door open, and her eyes snapped open. Suddenly she wasn't as sure.

"Cody!" She called.

He appeared in the doorway, coat in hand, looking back at her.

"Stay." She whispered the word, not certain whether he'd heard her or not.

Finally he drew a long, uneven breath. "You're sure?"

"No . . . no," she whispered. "I'm not sure of anything . . . except that I want you to stay— please . . ."

Dropping his coat on the floor, he walked across the room and pulled her into his arms. His fingers tangled in her hair as his mouth closed over hers, devouring, taking, seeking.

He lifted her, and Darby slipped her arms around his neck, allowing all of her doubts and fears to wash away on the tide of sensations filling her.

Hope, despair—love. She felt an incredible amount of emotions all tied together sweep through her.

"Where's your bed?" he whispered.

She pointed the way, her mouth refusing to leave his even for an instant.

They drifted down on the bed, their clothes melting away piece by agonizing piece. Their words jumbled together as passion began to build.

The need was more urgent than before, more overpowering, yet they longed to know each other, to hold each other, to say all the words they had been saving for each other.

Cody's mouth devoured hers, hot and demanding, filling her with wave after wave of mindless passion. She became fascinated with his body, all dark hair, muscle, and taut skin. She couldn't touch or taste or stroke or feel enough.

Sanity quickly gave way to abandonment. Gone was the shyness. Now they fed on each other's darker desires.

He rolled her beneath him and the sensations of flesh, growing moist and damp, exhilarated and drove them as murmurs became hot and incoherent.

Hands touched, explored, mindlessly familiarizing themselves.

Cody groaned as he felt his control slipping. He wanted more of her, more time to hold her to love her.

Moaning her name, he cupped her closer, feeling the passion contracting into an agonizing wall of flames.

"I love you," he whispered hoarsely.

Gasping his name, she couldn't answer, she could only reach for him as the ball of fire in her middle shattered into a million tiny, incredibly sweet, exquisite pieces.

Eight

Sighing, Darby lay against Cody's furred chest, limp, drained, and luminous.

A smile touched the corners of his mouth as he tenderly brushed the damp tendrils of hair back from her face. "We're going to have to do something about this."

"You didn't enjoy it?"

"I loved it. I'd just like for it to last a little longer than the speed of light."

Darby grinned, lifting her head to kiss him again. "Not my fault."

They kissed leisurely, basking in the warm afterglow.

"Marry me, and we'll devote our time to perfecting it," he coaxed in a soft whisper.

"No."

"Yes."

"Cody, please. Isn't it enough that you've worn me down until I'm ready to admit that I'm madly in love with you?"

"No, not nearly enough. I want all of you, Darby. All of you." Their mouths drifted back together and refused to part for a very long time.

"And you also want marriage and a family," she murmured.

"I do. Three kids—at least."

She groaned.

"Family is important to me, Darby. I want all the things the word stands for. Children, baseball games, tree houses, sandboxes, Santa Claus, sleigh rides, snowmen, snow ice cream, Boy Scouts, Camp Fire girls, dental bills, and chocolate chip cookies. I want the whole bit. I've just never found anyone I wanted to build that life with. Until now."

"Cody—"

"I know," he stopped her. "The lawsuit's in the way right now. But however it turns out, whether it's settled in my favor or yours, it won't affect how I feel about you. I'll do whatever the judge says."

"It honestly won't matter?"

"Well, sure—it'll matter to me. I hate to think people have grown so callous that they want to take away something that children enjoy so much.

After all, that's what Christmas is all about, isn't it? Love? And kids and all the dreams and hopes only a child can have."

"Yes." Tears stung her eyes. He was so filled with love that it hurt her to think she was part of a plan to stifle his generosity. Why did she have to be the attorney assigned to the *Haven Heights* case? Why couldn't it have been someone else? Someone who wouldn't fall in love with the defendant.

"So, whatever the verdict is," he said, shrugging, "we'll live through it."

"Even if it means taking the display down and never putting it up again?"

"Even if it means taking it down and never putting it up again. Cody shifted to rest on one elbow, smiling down at her. "I think I made a mistake. I should have hired you as my attorney."

"You think so, huh?"

"Yeah, I bet old McDonald runs a tight ship, but I'd put my money on you in the courtroom."

"Old McDonald graduated at the top of his class. I happen to know. Jeff and I were in the same graduating class," Darby pointed out.

"You were valedictorian," Cody said. "And Jeff was salutatorian."

"Uhhh . . . vice versa."

Cody shrugged. "Jeff must have cheated on one of his tests."

She grinned. "That's what I thought."

He leaned over and stole another kiss from her. "So, what's your preference?"

"Concerning what?"

"What do we want? Two boys and a girl, or two girls and a boy? Do you realize by this time next year we could be a family of three? Wouldn't that be great? We'll buy a huge house and put up a gigantic Christmas tree with all the trimmings. We'll invite both our families over for Christmas Eve and sing carols around the fireplace. Then at midnight we'll go to church. When we come back, you and I will exchange our gifts." The blue in his eyes deepened. "Then we'll make love—right there in front of the fireplace. . . ."

Darby closed her eyes. He was making it so difficult.

"Cody," she warned quietly.

"What do you think? Do you like two-story houses? I hate fighting the damn traffic, so maybe we should go—"

"Cody." She tried again.

"What?"

"I love you."

The change that came over his face made her heart ache. It was as if she'd given him the greatest gift imaginable. "I know—and I love you too," he whispered. Before she could go on, he drew her into his arms, and they kissed again.

"Cody, I do love you," she continued when their lips reluctantly parted.

His features grew serious. "Why do I imagine that I still hear a 'but' in there somewhere."

"Because you do." Her finger came up to trace his bottom lip lovingly. "I can't marry you—at least not right now . . . you know that."

"No, I don't know that."

"I've said it before."

"But that was before you admitted that you were in love with me."

"Falling in love and marriage are two entirely different things."

"Not to me. One follows the other."

"Cody, please understand. I didn't plan for this to happen."

"Do you have to *plan* everything? Can't you just let things *happen* for once?"

"No," she said stubbornly. "Maybe in two to three years—"

"Forget that."

"Oh, Cody." She wanted to shake him! *How* was she going to make him understand? "In two to three years I should be settled in the firm, my workload won't be as heavy, and I can begin to think about marriage and children—but not right now."

She could see he was going to argue with her.

"Look." She searched for a compromise. "Maybe . . . maybe we could try living together . . ." Her words faltered lamely when she saw the glacial look come into his eyes.

"You can forget that too. We either commit or we don't. I don't do things halfway."

Stung, Darby retorted, "Nor do I! That's why I can't seriously consider marriage right now. I'm dedicated to achieving my goal. I've worked hard. Harder than you can imagine. And I'm just about to reach the end of a long struggle. A full partnership with the firm. I can't divide my attention right now. I'm committed to my career and that means time. A great deal of it. Time I can't take away for a marriage or a family. Time I couldn't share with you. And I can't even *think* about having children. Children need time and patience, and when I'm working on a case, I have neither. It just wouldn't be fair."

"You think what you're doing to us is fair?"

She closed her eyes in frustration. "We just met at the wrong time," she said evenly.

"For you, maybe. I've been looking for you for a long time."

"Cody, please understand."

"Understand what? That your career is more important than me?"

He swung out of bed and started pulling his clothes on in angry jerks.

"No!" She got up and put on her robe. "It's not that it's more important, it's just that . . ." She wished she could find the right words. Words that would make him understand without hurting him. Hurting him was the last thing she wanted to do, but she didn't want to be hurt either. She pushed her fingers through her hair impatiently.

"There are just too many things in the way. I can't just up and get married. That isn't sensible."

"Love isn't meant to be sensible."

"But it has to be. I have to be sensible. I've worked for years—most of my life—toward achieving my goal." She resorted to pleading now. "And I've just about reached it. Cody, can't you even try to understand my dilemma? When I was twelve years old, I knew what I wanted to be. Everything in my life has been directed toward that. I can't just toss it all aside."

"I didn't ask you to. I've already said I'll support your career. I'll even volunteer to drive the car pool. What more can I do?"

"But it's more than my goals. We're at different stages in our lives. I mean, you've already established your company. You're ready to settle down. I've just bought this place and have a mortgage as big as the national debt, and an *almost* partnership in my law firm. But there are other things too. You're a happy-go-lucky, go-with-the-flow kind of guy, and I like to plan things to the nth degree and follow every rule. My hours are long and you're your own boss. Sometimes I don't get home until ten o'clock. I work on briefs all night and leave at seven the next morning. I can't ask you to put up with that kind of life."

"You didn't ask. I volunteered. And I'm getting

turned down." His gaze softened. "Has it ever occurred to you that my hours aren't exactly 'normal'? I'm at the office by seven, and sometimes I work past dark. As for me being my own boss, wrong, sweetheart, I write the checks, but without the customers I wouldn't be in business very long. All these roadblocks you're putting in our way can be worked out. If we want to work them out."

"Be fair, Cody. Darn it, you're allergic to cats, and I've had FurBall since I was *sixteen*. He's getting old! I couldn't put him out on the street."

"I can take pills for my allergies. I can't take pills and get over you," he replied tautly, pulling on his shirt and tucking the tails into his pants.

Darby watched him, her heart aching. She did love him. There was no doubt in her mind. But loving cost so much. And what if they married in haste, then they found out they'd made a mistake. Where would that leave her?

"I do love you," she said softly.

Cody stamped on his boots. "Well, actions sometimes speak louder than words."

She decided to try a different tack. "We hardly know one another."

"I don't feel as if I hardly know you." He paused, looking at her, his face set with determination. "When I hold you in my arms, I know you. When we're together, there's no doubt in my mind you're the woman I've waited for all my life. When we make love, it only strengthens my knowledge."

"Aren't you confusing sexual attraction with love?"

"No. I'm not. Are you?"

"I resent that."

"Then it's a moot question, isn't it, counselor?"

That stung. It really did. He was being unreasonable. Stubborn and unreasonable. He had his mind set on getting married, and he wasn't going to take "wait" for an answer.

He reached for his coat, then paused and turned back to face her. "By the way, Darby. How long have your parents been married?"

Darby met his gaze evenly. "Thirty-five years."

"Does your mother work outside the home?"

"Yes. She's had a small craft shop for years."

"A successful business?"

"Very. Mother is an intelligent and capable woman."

"How large a business is it?"

"It's a retail business. She has everything imaginable from wood crafts to fabrics, to flowers and hobby materials." Darby failed to understand his sudden interest in her parents.

"Does she do all the work herself or does she have people working for her?"

"I know what you're getting at, Cody. Yes, Mom is a successful businesswoman—but believe me, I came home to an empty house many times. When other children's mothers were home baking cookies, mine was out trying to make it in the business world. She did the best she could, but I want more than that for my children. I want to be there when they come home from school. I want to bake them those damn chocolate chip cookies that makes a child's youth so secure and memorable!"

"So, you didn't have chocolate chip cookies waiting for you each day. Has that left you with a warped view of society?"

"No."

"Then what's the sweat? Your mother has been married *thirty-five* years, raised three, I would venture to guess, pretty solid citizens in addition to running a successful business. All at the same time." He winked. "Think about it, sweetheart."

She understood what he was doing now. He was making her look like a fool. "It's not the same," she said coldly. "Today's women are forced to work, run a household, limousine service, emergency care unit, and never admit to being exhausted. Well, maybe I'm just not big enough to handle all of that effectively."

"Yes, you are. You just refuse to see it. Besides I already offered to run the limo service." He came over to her and tilted her face up to meet his. "Look, I'm thirty-eight years old. I've had relationships with women before. Enough of them to know that what you and I share is not going to go away. And I wouldn't propose to a woman and not have every intention of making the marriage work.

"Granted, there are no guarantees. But we'll work at it. Together. There might be times when you can't be there to meet the kids, but I can. Hell, I can bake cookies! Big, fat, chunky ones. You just have to trust, that between us, we can raise our children without one of them turning out to be a psychotic misfit."

He made everything sound so simple, but it wasn't. It was tremendously complicated. Why couldn't he just see that and give her more time.

"Marriage and family are important to me too, Cody. You're important to me. But I can't just decide on a whim to get married. I can't take a chance on making a mistake. I couldn't bear that. I don't want to be hurt, and I don't want you hurt. And I don't want my children hurt. I have to do things in the right order."

Cody drew a deep breath. "Then I guess we have a hung jury, counselor."

Darby swallowed back the lump crowding her throat. "Looks that way, doesn't it?"

He was leaving, and there was nothing she could say to make him stay. Nothing short of promising to marry him. And she refused to be driven to that point.

And yet she couldn't let him go—not like this.

"Cody, look . . . can't we think about this?" Her

heart was in her eyes now. And her love. She didn't want him to leave angry.

"Sorry. You want to compromise what we feel for one another. I'm not a compromising man. I'm an all-or-nothing kind of guy when it comes to matters of the heart. I hoped you'd realized that."

He turned, and she trailed behind him to the door. "Cody . . . maybe I could cut the time down to only a year . . . that isn't very long. . . ."

He opened the door, then hesitated. Hope sprang inside her. He turned and she reached out to touch his face, hoping for at least a good-bye kiss. But he only bent and brushed her forehead absently. "See you around, kiddo."

Then after a brief caress to her cheek, he swung the door open, stepped out, and closed it firmly behind him.

Darby stood stunned for a moment, unable to believe he'd really left. When she heard the Bronco start a few moments later, then back out of the drive, she dropped to the floor on her knees and began to sob.

Nine _____

Darby turned over a page in her calendar book and stared at it listlessly. December 22. Two days before Christmas Eve, and she'd never felt less in the holiday spirit. Her mother had called that morning to discuss plans for Christmas and had asked if Darby had all her shopping finished; Darby had almost burst into tears. She was miserable. She hadn't heard a word from Cody, and she knew that she wouldn't. The first move would have to come from her. She'd almost picked up the phone a dozen times.

But at least she'd be seeing him today. The litigants were to meet this morning at nine.

The telephone buzzed and Darby reached for it. "The Kinnitses have arrived," Gail said.

"Put them in the conference room, and let me know when Mr. Benderman and his attorney arrive."

"They're just coming in."

"Thank you. I'll be right there."

The beginnings of a tension headache nagged at the base of her skull. She was exhausted, she hadn't slept the past few nights. Trying to force Cody out of her thoughts, she'd made an attempt to bury herself in work, yet she'd not slept a full night since he'd left. All she wanted to do was curl up in some corner and hide.

She took two aspirins, picked up the *Haven Heights* file, and stood up. She straightened her shoulders in an effort to appear professional even though she felt light-years away from her work.

She strode down the hallway and hesitated at the door of the conference room, trying to steel herself against seeing Cody again. When she opened the door, his was the first face she saw.

He was wearing a tobacco-brown suit that had to be a Bill Blass, a cream-colored shirt, and a patterned tie. He was already seated, looking like someone out of *Gentlemen's Quarterly*—successful, confident, handsome.

But on second glance she noticed that he looked extremely tired too. And she couldn't detect even a hint of a smile of welcome. Her spirits sank even lower. She might have found a compromise for the lawsuit, but there would be no compromise between them personally.

As he'd said, he was an all-or-nothing kind of guy.

"Darby," Jeff said, offering his hand.

"Jeff." She clasped his hand in greeting.

She nodded to the Kinnitses, and as she turned to Cody, their eyes met.

"Good morning, Mr. Benderman."

"Good morning, Ms. Piper."

Oh, Lord. How could she sit here in this small room with him and retain her composure!

Calmly taking her place at the head of the table, she drew a deep breath.

"I know you're wondering why I've requested this meeting."

"Well, we certainly are," Arvilla sniffed. "Louis and I thought everything was ready for court. I bought a new dress."

"Court is set for day after tomorrow," Darby soothed, "but I hope after this morning we won't have need to proceed any further." She looked up and tried to smile. "I hope I have an agreeable solution to the problem. At least, I feel it is worthy of consideration."

"A compromise?" Jeff asked.

"Perhaps."

"What is it?"

Darby was aware that Cody still hadn't spoken.

But she also knew that his gaze had never left her.

"I took it upon myself to approach the city with an idea, and I'm pleased to say they've agreed to it."

"What idea?" Arvilla edged forward on her chair.

"Now, dear, let Miss Piper talk," Louis said, patting his wife's hand appeasingly. "I'll listen to anything that will keep us out of court on Christmas Eve."

"But we can't cave in, Louis," Arvilla whispered. "Our neighbors are depending on us."

"No one's caving in, sugarcakes. Go on, Miss Piper. Tell us what you have in mind."

Darby's fingertips came up absently to massage her temples. She glanced over at Cody; he was still watching her.

Stop looking at me or I'll lose it, she pleaded silently.

"I've spoken to the park board about having Mr. Benderman's display be put on in a small city park," she began. "They were delighted with the idea. There is a suitable park midtown, and people would be able to drive either around it or through it. Mr. Benderman's decorations could be set up in sections and displayed each year for all of Boston's enjoyment."

Jeff whistled softly beneath his breath. "I like it."

Chancing another brief glance at Cody, Darby

saw that his gaze was still fixed on her. If he didn't go for the compromise, she didn't know what she would do. She couldn't go to court against him. She knew she couldn't argue the case convincingly. And it was too late to turn the case over to someone else even if she'd wanted to. If this plan didn't work, she was beaten.

"Additions to the display could easily be made. People could get out and walk around the displays, listen to the music, or simply drive through and enjoy the scenes. The Salvation Army wants to have a strolling band in the small square."

"That sounds great," Jeff said. "What do you think, Cody?"

Cody's eyes remained on Darby. "Whatever Ms. Piper has arranged is fine with me."

Darby forced herself to remain professional. But she felt a strong urge to hug him. Actually, she wanted to do much more than hug him, but for the moment hugging would have helped.

"Thank you, Mr. Benderman."

"You're welcome, Ms. Piper."

"Well, now. I think it sounds like a real good solution," Louis said. "What do you think, dear?"

Arvilla considered the idea carefully, her mouth pursed and a frown creasing her forehead. "I . . . well, actually I like it, Louis. It sounds fair to me."

"The City of Boston will store the decorations, but I have arranged for Mr. Benderman to retain the option of taking care of the construction and dismantling each year. Any additions he feels are needed will have to be cleared through the park board, but they're very appreciative of this opportunity. In fact, they told me that they've been considering such a display but hadn't decided how to obtain the necessary funding." She chanced another brief glance at Cody. He was watching her closely, but his look seemed oddly impersonal. "Okay with you, Mr. Benderman?" she asked softly.

"Okay with me, Ms. Piper," he said.

"Mr. and Mrs. Kinnits? Will you recommend to your neighbors that they accept the compromise?"

"We'll call them as soon as we get home. You'll have our answer by the morning, if not sooner," Arvilla said. "Isn't that right, Louis?"

"That's right, dear." Louis stood and reached to shake Darby's hand. "Miss Piper, thank you for all of your help. I'm sure this will be just fine with our neighbors, don't you think so, Arvilla?"

"I wouldn't presume to speak for our neighbors, Louis, but I certainly find the solution quite acceptable. You'll be hearing from us by no later than tomorrow afternoon."

Relieved, Darby closed the file. "Then as soon as I hear from the Kinnitses, I'll phone you with the response, Jeff. Any more questions?"

When there were none, Darby stood up. "Then let's all hope we can be home with our families on Christmas Eve."

Her gaze moved unwillingly back to Cody's, and the look on his face made her wince. It clearly said that if he had his way, they would be married on Christmas Eve.

"Darby, good work," Jeff complimented. "I was hoping something could be worked out."

"I'm delighted it's turned out this way," she said. "The main purpose of Mr. Benderman's display is to bring happiness. Now even more people will be able to enjoy Mr. Benderman's idea of the true spirit of Christmas."

Jeff followed the Kinnitses out of the conference room, leaving Darby and Cody alone briefly.

Cody stood for a moment, and his fingertips rested lightly on the tabletop.

Darby watched him from the corner of her eye, wishing there was something she could say to end their impasse. But she remained silent, and when she glanced up a few moments later, he was looking at her.

"Thanks," he said.

"For what?"

"For finding a compromise."

A lump formed in her throat again. "I thought you didn't like compromises."

His gaze was direct, and there was not much warmth in it. She longed for him to smile, longed to see that twinkle of mischief in his eyes again. But what she saw now was only a resigned acceptance. Her heart ached. She'd caused that look.

"I don't mind compromise in business. Just not in my personal life. You see, I have priorities too," he reminded her.

"I know." Her gaze dropped, unable to meet his now.

"Well . . . I just wanted to say, merry Christmas, darling."

"Merry Christmas," she whispered brokenly.

As the door closed behind him, Darby sank back onto her chair and closed her eyes.

Everyone said love was so wonderful.

Why had no one ever bothered to mention that it could hurt so much?

By the end of the day her headache was worse. Darby decided she wouldn't wait for the Kinnitses' call any longer. She left the office at six and started home.

The air was filled with the sounds and feel of Christmas. People scurried about from last-minute shopping, laden with gaily wrapped packages. Store windows were resplendent with decorations and all the follies that people were tempted to overspend on.

Ordinarily, Darby loved the Christmas season. People seemed more polite and ready to laugh or call greetings to complete strangers. But she knew that come the first of January, the majority would revert back to their normal selves.

Snow was threatening again as she pulled her car into the garage. Catching sight of the red sled, she was tempted to drive out to Rudman's Hill, but decided that would be foolish. It would only remind her of Cody.

She opened her mailbox and found it stuffed with Christmas greetings. The bold scrawls reminded her of the night she and Cody had addressed her cards.

And the night they'd first made love.

As she walked into her house she didn't fight the tears any longer. They rolled unchecked down her cheeks as she sat down on the couch. Even FurBall's best attempts to comfort her failed. She could only remember how comical Cody had looked when he'd first seen the cat and started to sneeze, and how nice he'd been to say he could always take allergy pills if necessary.

Isn't that what it took? she reminded herself. A willingness to give up some part of yourself for another person. Wasn't that what love was all about? Sharing, making adjustments, feeling concern more for the one you love than for your own wants and needs.

It didn't make sense. None of it did. She *was* in love with Cody. She was certain of that now. But if she loved him, why couldn't she make adjustments in her life for him? Other women had careers and families. And they survived. The men in the firm had families. But they'd already carved their niche, she argued. They'd already achieved the goal that was eluding her. A full partnership. She couldn't just throw away a dream, could she?

She closed her eyes and wished she could just make everything easy again. There was a time when she'd been happy. And not that long ago. Before she'd met Cody.

But had she *really* been happy then? Hadn't being with Cody made her realize how one-dimensional her life had been? She fumbled for a tissue to blow her nose. Nothing was right anymore. Nothing made sense anymore. She'd lain awake thinking night after night trying to find a way to feel good about refusing his proposal.

Finally, she shrugged out of her coat and threw it over the arm of a chair, scattering Christmas cards across the floor. Leaving them, she stepped out of her boots and padded in her stocking feet into the kitchen.

FurBall followed closely, looking worried about her.

Opening the refrigerator door, Darby stared at the nearly empty interior. She'd forgotten to buy groceries. The only thing in there was a half-empty package of wieners and a quart of milk. Absently, she took a wiener out of the package and stuck it into her mouth. Closing the refrigerator door with her hip, she walked over and slumped down onto a kitchen chair, staring at the phone. Ring, darn you, she commanded silently. *Ring.*

She jumped when it did ring.

She snatched up the receiver breathlessly. "Hello?"

"Darling, I was just checking what time you'd be driving up."

Darby sank back onto her chair. "Nothing's changed, Mother; I'm coming Christmas Eve, just as soon as I can get away from the office."

"Oh . . . can't you come sooner? I thought we could have some time to ourselves before the others get here. I'm worried about you, darling. You didn't sound yourself the other day."

"I'm fine, Mom."

"You don't sound fine. You sound unhappy. Are you unhappy?"

Depend on mother to read between the lines, she thought. "I just have things on my mind. I'm fine."

"You're not. But if you don't want to talk about it now, we won't. We can talk when you get home. We'll take some extra time during the holidays to chat, just like we used to. And you drive carefully. The weatherman's predicting snow again."

"I will, Mom. See you in a couple of days."

Darby hung up the phone and glumly took another bite of the cold wiener.

"FurBall, you're right. This is revolting." She tossed the rest of the wiener into the trash can.

Forcing herself to do something, Darby opened her Christmas cards and added them to the others, which had nearly filled the large coffee table. She turned on the television for company and almost turned it off when a commercial for "Christmas for Him" came on and the male model reminded her of Cody. Actually, everything she looked at reminded her of Cody.

"This is crazy. Snap out of it!"

She decided to wrap Christmas presents and forced herself to stay with the job until it was finished. Usually she enjoyed making the bows and creating special wrappings, but this year it just didn't hold the same thrill. But it did manage to fill the time until nearly midnight when she forced herself to drag upstairs.

After a hot shower Darby lay in her bed wide awake in spite of the sleeping pill she'd taken.

Each time she closed her eyes, Cody's face floated into her mind. His face, with a disappointed look. His face, with an impish grin. His face, with its strong planes softened by love.

Almost like probing a new wound, she remembered Cody as Santa Claus, picketing the front of her building. The night he'd come over to light the pilot light and just happened to have a pizza in his Bronco. She'd been so tired that night, so strung out, and he'd understood her frustrations. And who else but Cody would have thrown a snowball at her or taken her sledding? No one.

Everyone knew she was too . . . stuffy . . . to get into a snowball fight, didn't they? Oh, not Miss Priss Darby Piper. She was always so proper.

But with Cody she wasn't like that. With Cody she laughed and giggled like a schoolgirl. She'd made snowballs and thrown them back at him, never giving a thought to how it might affect her image. And certainly no one would ever have thought she'd be caught sledding. But it had been wonderful. Wonderfully spontaneous and fun. Cody was the only one she would have done something like that with. Only Cody.

Cody, who wanted a wife, a home, and children to give his love to. Tears dampened her eyes again. Wonderfully warm and gentle and loving Cody. Cody, who loved children and who wanted to have three of his own. Cody, who wanted her to be the mother of those children.

But dare she throw caution to the wind and accept his proposal? They'd known one another only *four* weeks. And they'd spent the first two weeks growling at one another about a bulldozer. A woman just didn't toss away a lifetime of plans and dreams for someone she'd met only a month ago, did she?

Some people do. If they're in love.

Hadn't her parents told their daughters dozens of times that you couldn't dictate love? *They'd* fallen in love at nineteen and married within a month. Darby recalled how they always ended the story by gazing fondly at one another and vowing that neither of them had ever had a moment's regret.

Darby sighed and rolled onto her side. She was in love with Cody, wasn't she? Hopelessly in love?

Yes, yes, yes!

She'd tried telling herself she wasn't, but the words echoed back falsely. She couldn't forget him, and she didn't want to let him go.

And Cody was in love with her, wasn't he? Yes, he was. She had to believe he was. No one, not even Cody Benderman, went around asking women to marry him just on a whim. Family meant too much to him. She could see that in everything he said and did.

Then what was the problem? Her. Her and her career. So, she asked herself the ultimate question in her most officious manner: *Is your career that important to you?*

Yes, she returned. *Yes! Yes!*

It wasn't as if she'd just woken up one day last year and decided that maybe a full partnership in one of the most prestigious law firms in the city might be a fun thing. She'd been working toward this point in her life for the past twelve years. It was something she'd expected of herself. It had been the focal point of her entire adult life. Becoming a full partner in the firm would mean that all her hard work and sacrifices had meant something.

But didn't marriage and family mean something? Something every bit as important as a career? Maybe Cody was right. Her mother *had* raised a family and had managed a rewarding career at the same time. Her mother had become interested in crafts about the time Darby had entered elementary school, and she had only begun the craft shop when Darby had entered high school, but the venture had been demanding.

Darby remembered the nights her mother had sat up finishing a special project or working on the accounts. No one in the family had thought anything about it. Only now did Darby appreciate how much time and effort her mother had put into work. It hadn't been easy for her mother, Darby realized now. She and her sisters had been typical teenagers. They'd fought as much as they'd laughed among themselves. Mother was an independent woman, and her father had always appreciated that in his wife. He'd always been the sort of husband who helped with the household chores and shared the responsibility for raising his daughters, though he often admitted he didn't understand them at all. But there had been love. Not many home-baked cookies, but lots of love. And sharing. Only after she'd gone to college had Darby realized how much love and care had gone into her raising. Couldn't she summon the same grit as her parents had? Couldn't she take time to give her child the values the way her parents had given them to her?

Yes, she could.

So, what's the problem, counselor?

She loved Cody. No problem there. Didn't she think he meant what he said about appreciating her abilities as a career woman and supporting her dreams? Yes, she believed that he did. And shouldn't he be able to expect the same from her? Of course. And she would give him one hundred percent *because* she loved him.

She rolled back to stare at the ceiling. Still, she couldn't argue away the fact that they hadn't known each other very long. Divorce statistics were frightening enough without the added burden of two demanding careers in the same house. Given the added responsibility of children, it could result in disaster, couldn't it?

But do you want children?

Yes!

Now?

The answer was slower in coming. *No . . .* not now . . . yet her biological clock was ticking. She was thirty-two. If she ever planned to have children, she should at least be thinking about it soon. She wanted to be young enough to enjoy them. She fondly recalled trips to the zoo and picnics and box seats at the circus where her mother and father ate sticky cotton candy along with their girls and laughed at the antics of the clowns. She wanted that for her children. She wanted the time to spend with them, enjoy them, and she wanted her partnership too.

She drew a deep sigh. There seemed to be no answers. What she needed was for someone to just tell her what to do and guarantee it was the right thing.

She glanced at the clock. Four A.M. She'd never be able to get through the next day if she didn't get some sleep.

Rolling over, she drew the pillow close to her, cradling it in her arms. Her imagination told her Cody's cologne still clung to the pillowcase, and her closed eyes smarted with tears again.

Oh, Cody, why couldn't we have met two years from now. Or even three months from now when I might already have the partnership. Why now?

Ten

Christmas Eve day arrived with fresh snow, crisp air, and bright sunshine. Church bells rang over the city. The air seemed to tingle with excitement and anticipation.

Darby parked the BMW in front of C.B. Construction and walked inside. There was no one at the reception desk, so she tapped lightly on a door marked C. BENDERMAN, then opened it.

Cody glanced up, surprise crossing his handsome features.

"Hi, Benderman," she said.

"Hi, Piper."

Coming to his feet, Cody watched as she pulled off her mittens and coat and laid them across a chair. The wind had tossed her hair and kissed her cheeks a rosy red. She looked so beautiful that he couldn't take his eyes off her.

Calmly she began to stroll around the room, studying it, absorbing its tone. This was where Cody spent much of his time, and it clearly reflected his taste. It was the kind of office she loved: rich walnut paneling, cinnamon-colored carpeting, a wide walnut desk, and comfortable side chairs covered in a lush, tweedy fabric in cinnamon, brown, and persimmon. The drapes were the same cinnamon color, and the pictures were mostly pastoral scenes. A tall cabinet was open, revealing slots for blueprints, all neatly labeled. There was a matching bookcase filled to overflowing with books of all shapes and sizes. The room looked warm and inviting. Just like the man.

"This is nice. Much nicer than my chrome and glass."

"I like it."

"I've always hated the decor in my office." She shrugged. "Once I become a full partner, I'm going to complain." Her gaze met his and she grinned.

"Something on your mind?" he asked.

She could see that he was wondering why she was in his office making small talk. It was probably a silly thing to do, coming here like this, but she'd made a lot of mistakes in her relationship with Cody thus far. So another one more or less couldn't make much difference at this point.

Darby seated herself in one of the chairs in front of his desk. "I heard you were looking for volunteers to help deliver Christmas gifts to the hospital this evening."

"Oh?" His left eyebrow raised. "Where did you hear that?"

"Oh, some little angel whispered it to me."

Actually, she'd done a little investigating after hearing a piece on the morning news about how Cordell Benderman was sponsoring the annual Christmas party at the hospital Christmas Eve. She also discovered that Cody would be very involved in the party: He would play Santa for the children.

"I'm here to volunteer my services," she said.

She waited, trying to gauge his reaction. He had every right to tell her to leave. She couldn't blame him. He'd handed her his heart, and she'd handed it right back to him. He had a right to be hurt, deeply hurt, even if he had understood her reasoning. She wasn't even sure that she understood it . . . entirely.

"Are you an elf now?" he teased.

There was a long pause as their gazes caught and held. "I am if you want me to be," she said softly. She would be anything he wanted her to be.

Cody sat back down. Picking up a pencil, he

studied it. The silence lengthened, and Darby felt panic rising in her throat.

"Well," he finally said, "I never refuse a helping hand. People are generous with their money but not with their time. It takes a good deal of effort to get the gifts wrapped and then get them to the hospital, let alone hand them out and spend a little time with each child."

She was a little disappointed by his detachment but not surprised. He had a right to be wary.

"When will you be delivering the gifts?"

"This evening, about six." His looked at her, assessingly. "Will that be convenient?"

"Yes." She would call her mother and tell her that her plans had changed and that she wouldn't be home until Christmas Day.

"It won't interfere with your holiday plans?"

"Not at all."

His gaze ran over her lightly again before returning to the papers littering his desk. "You might want to bring a change of clothes. We'll be at the hospital all evening, so we'll grab a sandwich on the way home."

"Sure. Sounds great." She deliberately matched her tone to his. She already knew what she would wear. The red wool dress. If she was going to throw herself at him, she'd do it in style.

"I'll pick you up about five-thirty, and we'll go directly to the hospital."

"Fine." She stood. She longed to say more yet

was hesitant. He hadn't smiled. "See you at five-thirty."

"Um-hmm," he dismissed absently, already reading the blueprints again.

Darby left C.B. Construction and headed straight for a costume shop.

She'd wipe that indifference from his tone.

And fast.

When the doorbell rang that evening, Darby glanced in the mirror and gave one last yank to her costume before answering.

Opening the door, she found Cody on the step, resplendent in his Santa costume.

He opened his mouth, then shut it again, his eyes summarizing her costume.

She'd been lucky. The costume shop had a large selection to choose from. She'd rushed home after a short day at the office, showered quickly, and put on the red dress. Brushing her hair back, she'd slipped on a white wig, which she drew back and pinned into a bun at the nape of her neck. A white bib apron, red shoes, and little wire-rim glasses perched on the end of her nose completed her costume, transforming her into a more-svelte-than-usual Mrs. Claus.

She slowly turned around for his inspection, smugly noting the way his eyes had suddenly grown darker. "You like?"

"Yeah . . . I like. Ready?"

She felt a twinge of disappointment. She'd been sure the dress would do the trick. Darby handed him her cape. He draped it about her shoulders, and they walked silently to the Bronco, which was filled to overflowing with packages.

"Cody . . . there are so many!" Darby exclaimed. "How will we get them all into the hospital?"

"The staff will help. I have Santa bags to put the packages in before we go into each ward."

Darby began to wonder if she was doing the right thing. In her eagerness to mend bridges, she hadn't thought this through very well. Until this moment she had not realized they'd be seeing and talking to children in all stages of recovery. Some might be very sick. She loved children so much she wasn't sure she could be optimistic and filled with Christmas cheer in the face of such sadness.

Cody held the door open for her. "Coming?"

"Coming," she murmured.

"Well, at least it's not snowing," she said as they drove to the hospital, trying to ease the strained silence. She was trying not to babble, but she didn't know how to tell him that she had changed her mind. After last night her priorities had altered. Not changed, just altered. She realized now that she wanted everything—a career and a marriage. With a man like Cody the two would compliment each other.

"Darby, what's this all about?"

She tensed. Cody's voice sounded harsh. "I just thought you might need some help."

He turned and looked at her, his features illuminated under the passing streetlights. "I do. But I need you more."

Well, here it was, the opening she had been waiting for. He had made the first move toward reconciliation. He was giving her the chance to say what was in her heart. She swallowed, then started to speak, only to discover that FurBall must have stolen her tongue.

"Well?" he prompted softly.

"Well . . . I like you too," she returned lamely, then wished the floorboard would open up and swallow her.

He turned and looked at her again, a smile tugging at the corners of his mouth. "Yeah?"

"Yeah," she said, her eyes returning his smile.

Two nurses were waiting to help with the packages as Cody pulled the Bronco to the entry of the children's wing of the hospital.

A half hour later the packages were all separated and in "Santa's bags." They rode up in the elevator together, the nurses' chatter about how much the children were anticipating Santa's visit filling the silence.

For the next three hours Darby saw through Cody's eyes what Christmas was really all about.

Cody was a natural charmer, and he moved easily from one bed to the next, captivating the patients. He had a soft word for each child, a gentle touch, and lots of ho-ho-hos to set the more ambulatory ones giggling with glee. The nurses whispered a name and something about each child's injury as they approached each bed, so "Santa" could "know everything naughty and nice" about them.

Darby's heart went out to each one, and she wished that somehow she could take away their pain and make them feel carefree again.

Little Gary was an imp with his glowing brown eyes and a wide grin with its gap where his two front teeth had been. He'd been riding his bike when he'd been hit by a car. As a result, he had three cracked ribs and one leg in traction.

The nurses had tied a big red bow on the cables holding his leg in the air, and the foot of his bed sported a large knitted stocking. Darby thought an Etch-A-Sketch from Santa would provide hours of distraction.

Then there was little, shy Ann with her saucer-like, blue eyes and angel-fine hair who waited patiently in her bed until Santa reached her.

"And what's your name?" Cody boomed.

"Ann Elithabeth," she lisped in a reverent whisper.

The little girl had an arm and a leg in a cast as the result of an automobile accident. Darby longed to take her in her arms and hug her.

"Well, well, Santa has something special in his bag for you." Cody grinned, reaching out to touch her pale cheek. "Mrs. Claus? Don't we have something in the bag with Ann Elithabeth's name on it?"

"Why, yes, Nicholas. I believe we have." Darby pulled an oblong package out of Santa's bag and handed it to Cody.

"Here you go, darlin'. This should keep you company while you're here and later while you're home getting well again." He placed the package in her lap. "I bet Mrs. Claus would help you open that."

Darby sat on the edge of the bed, ready to be of service. "I'll hold this end of the ribbon, and you pull that end," she directed.

Ann glanced up with an embarrassed smile, but pulled the ribbon until it came loose.

Cody watched the two of them. Darby had been wonderful with the kids, smiling and laughing at their delighted shrieks as they opened each package.

Cody shook his head with amazement, recalling how one particular little boy had clung to Darby, not wanting her to leave, and how she'd sat for a long time, holding him in her arms while the nurses helped Santa hand out the other packages. Darby was wonderful with the children.

She'd rocked the little toddler in a chair beside his bed, her chin resting on his shiny dark hair, tears sparkling in her eyes, until he'd fallen asleep.

The nurses had explained how the little boy missed his mother, who had died in the same accident that had nearly taken his life.

As Cody had watched Darby holding the child, who clutched his new teddy bear, he knew he would wait for her. She would be his wife no matter how long it took to persuade her.

One year, two years, or ten. She was the only one he wanted.

"Oh, look what Santa brought you." Darby smiled down at Ann Elizabeth, drawing Cody's attention back to the moment.

"A baby!" the little girl exclaimed in her whispery voice.

And indeed it was. An exquisitely lifelike baby doll in a pale-yellow nightgown with a bottle. The little girl cradled the doll awkwardly, unable to hold it properly with her arm in the cast.

"Here, put her like this; then you can feed her when she's hungry," Darby suggested, placing the 'baby' in the crook of Ann's cast, so she could hold the baby bottle with her uninjured hand.

Ann gave Darby a beatific smile, causing Darby to smile in return. She glanced up to find Cody watching her. His smile was warm and loving, and Darby's heart swelled with pride.

Cody was the most compassionate, warmhearted man she'd ever met. She couldn't picture any of the men she worked with in the law firm spending their Christmas Eve in the hospital with sick children.

"Well, little Ann, do you promise to take good care of your baby?" Santa asked.

"I promise," the little girl said, nodding solemnly.

"Good. She's a very special baby, and I knew the moment I saw you that you'd be exactly the kind of mother she needed."

Darby gave the little girl one last hug, then moved on to hand out the rest of the gifts. Though there were other children who reached inside her heart and touched her deeply, the memory of Ann's face remained with her.

It was almost nine-thirty when they finished. The nurses had prepared punch and cookies in the lounge, so Darby and Cody joined them for a few minutes. Darby sat on a small couch, toying with a cookie, thinking. She'd never experienced anything like this before.

Coming here tonight hadn't been what she'd expected. She'd thought they'd hand out gifts, say a few words to each child, and go on. But it hadn't been that way at all.

It was as if each child was her own. Hers and Cody's.

Each child had received his gift as if it were the very thing he wanted most in the world.

"Tired?"

Cody sat down beside her, relaxing for a moment. His beard was lopsided, and his cherry-red nose hung on a string around his neck now.

"A little." She thought a moment. " 'Stunned' is perhaps a better word. I didn't think I'd feel this way."

He glanced down at her. "How's that?"

"So . . . oh, you know—maternal."

He shrugged. "Nothing wrong in feeling maternal. Not at our age."

"No . . . guess not. Actually, I sort of like it."

Her hand slipped into his, and they shared the silence a moment.

"You hungry?"

"Um-hmm." Darby handed him her empty cup.

They walked to the elevator, arm in arm.

"Cody," a voice called.

Darby glanced up to find a pretty young nurse hurrying down the hallway.

"Hi," she greeted him breathlessly. Her large, liquid blue eyes ran up and down Cody hungrily. "Just wanted to remind you that I'm having the New Year's party at my place again. Hope you can come."

Cody's eyes twinkled mischievously as they met Darby's over the nurse's head. "Thanks, Sharon . . . I'll let you know."

The door to the elevator opened, and Darby and Cody stepped inside the small car.

"Was that the Sharon?"

"The Sharon?"

"Sharon of the Christmas-card Sharon," Darby clarified, wishing her jealousy weren't quite so evident.

" 'Sharon of the Christmas-card Sharon'? Oh, yeah . . . I believe it was." He grinned. "How did you know?"

"Lucky guess."

The bell tinged, and the door opened. As she walked across the lobby, Darby continued under her breath, "I suppose this New Year's party is an annual event?"

"Sort of."

"And I suppose you're usually her date?"

"Sort of—and I suppose you're going to a New Year's party with one of the Christmas-card men. Jeff or Jacques or Robert?"

"Might be," she returned smugly.

When they stepped outside snow was falling again. Cody took her arm to protect her from slipping on the slick pavement as they picked their way across the parking lot to the Bronco.

He walked her around to the passenger side, but instead of opening the door he suddenly paused. Turning her, he pressed her against the car.

Startled, Darby looked up to find his determined blue gaze pinpointing hers.

"Look, I'm asking you one more time. Will you marry me?"

Darby sagged with relief. "And I'm telling you one last time . . . I will."

"You will?" he asked. He looked dazed. He drew her closer. "When? One year—two? One I can stand, but two, now that's pushing it, Darby. We can surely—"

Covering his mouth with her hand, she muffled his flow of words. "No, right now. Tonight if you want."

"Tonight?" he repeated dazedly.

"Tonight."

"As much as I would like for that to happen, I don't see how it's possible. We have to have a license—"

Her hand came up to cover his mouth again. "Hey, you happen to be talking to someone who has a few connections with judges, remember?"

Cody drew her closer, their breaths mingling in the frosty air. "Oh, yeah? You've taken care of things?"

"Yeah, do you mind, Benderman?"

His mouth closed over hers, assuring her that he didn't. Not in the least.

"I love you," he murmured huskily.

"And I love you back," she whispered. Which she did. With all her heart.

*   *   *

Thirty minutes later they were ringing the doorbell of a house in the suburbs. The sign out front stated J. PETERSEN, JUSTICE OF THE PEACE.

"Are you sure he's expecting us?" Cody asked, skeptical.

"Positive. He's a personal friend of Bill Moorhouse."

"Judge William 'Give 'em Hell' Moorhouse? The one who has you buffaloed?"

"Ah, ole Billy's not so tough." She grinned. "By the way, he said to wish you good luck."

"Yeah?"

"Yeah . . . he said you were going to need it."

The door opened, and J. Petersen gaped at the sight of Mr. and Mrs. Claus standing on his porch.

"Well, well." He smiled. "What can I do for you two?"

"We want to get married," Cody said.

"And high time," J. Petersen quipped with a twinkle in his eye. "Come on in," he invited. "Martha," he called out. "You'll never *guess* who wants to get married."

A woman bustled in from the kitchen. "Oh, my," she exclaimed, eyeing Darby's and Cody's costumes.

"If we could borrow your bathroom, we'd both

like to change clothes before the ceremony," Cody said.

Martha beamed with relief. "Of course, it's just down the hall, Santa."

Cody turned to Darby, stealing another brief kiss. "You can change first."

"Oh, that's not necessary, I'll just take off my wig and these glasses," Darby said, untying the apron. She'd dressed with just this moment in mind. "If you have somewhere I can check my makeup?"

"Right this way." Mrs. Petersen directed her to a small bath adjacent to the living room.

Darby quickly ran a comb through her hair and freshened her makeup, wondering if she should have chosen something more traditional for her wedding dress. After all, she was only going to do this once—maybe twice if they decided to have a church service later.

But she realized the dress didn't matter. The man did. And she had the perfect one.

By the time she returned to the living room Cody had changed into a dark suit and tie. He looked breathtakingly handsome.

Going into each other's arms, they kissed, oblivious of the judge and his wife standing by with amused smiles.

"We're not even married yet, and you're already driving me crazy," she murmured.

He drew her closer, his eyes adoring her. "Just so I'm always the one in the driver's seat."

"You will be. I love you," she said softly.

"I love you."

"Uh-hump," the judge said, clearing his throat.

Darby broke the embrace, flushing. "I think we're holding up the ceremony."

"Shall we begin?"

"Whenever you're ready, Judge," Cody said.

"Martha, please?"

Mrs. Petersen seated herself at the old spinet piano. Darby couldn't remember the name of the tune she began to play, but it was an old English song, executed beautifully.

The music faded away, and the judge began reverently, "Dearly beloved, we have come together . . ."

Darby stood there with Cody, holding his hand and realizing that this was exactly where she wanted to be, with the man she wanted to spend her life with. Whatever doubts she'd had once were now forgotten.

She glanced up and smiled at the man who had come into her life so unexpectedly—an in such an unusual manner—and saw a similar expression of devotion in his eyes.

This was what it was all about.

Love, deep and abiding love.

It was the best Christmas present in the world.

Epilogue

Snow was falling softly outside the window.

Santa was busy zipping up and down chimneys, leaving traces of cookie crumbs on the plates in the houses he'd visited.

Christmas lights twinkled merrily, and somewhere in the distance a dog barked.

Snow White had stopped skating about an hour ago.

Mickey and Minnie each had one leg suspended in the air now, smiles permanently fixed on their wooden faces.

Rudolph's nose was no longer glowing.

The live animals were tucked safely away in a real stable for the night.

But beyond the yard that had caused so much

commotion, Cody and Darby lay in Cody's bed—their bed now—and toasted this very special, magical night.

"What changed your mind about marrying me?" Cody murmured, lifting his glass to toast his bride.

"You." The glasses met, making a tinkling sound.

He smiled, leaning forward to steal another long, slow kiss from his bride. His hand found her breast, caressing it gently. "How did I do that?"

"After you left the other night, I did a lot of thinking about everything you'd said. About us. And I finally realized that I couldn't base my life on what anyone else does or has done. I have to set my own rules. And I discovered that I am a romantic at heart. As long as we truly love each other, then I'm confident that we can work things out."

"Now, see. That's exactly what I've been trying to tell you."

"Now, see," she said good-naturedly, "don't start bossing me. I'm not the bossing type," she warned. Then she gave him a kiss to show that she could bend—a little. And maybe sometimes he could boss her—but only occasionally.

He smiled, taking her glass and setting it aside. "You know I'd never want to stand in the way of your career. I don't want you giving up anything to be with me. Together, we'll be more than we could be alone."

She sighed, settling back in his arms. They had made love, but the hunger was building again. She wondered if it would always be this way, and somehow she knew that it would.

"You know, *you're* a romantic, Cody Benderman."

He turned her in his arms and lowered his mouth to nuzzle her neck. "Well, Mrs. Benderman," he said, laying her back on the pillow and placing soft kisses along her neck. "if I am, you've made me one."

In the hallway the clock chimed midnight. It was Christmas Day, a day for new beginnings.

"Merry Christmas, Cody," she whispered.

"Merry Christmas, Darby. And a most happy and prosperous New Year."

THE EDITOR'S CORNER

It's a pleasure to return to the Editor's Corner while Susann Brailey is away on maternity leave, the proud mother of her first child—a beautiful, big, healthy daughter. It is truly holiday season here with this wonderful addition to our extended "family," and I'm delighted to share our feelings of blessings with you . . . in the form of wonderful books coming your way next month.

First, let me announce that what so many of you have written to me asking for will be in your stockings in just thirty days! Four classic LOVESWEPT romances from the spellbinding pen of Iris Johansen will go on sale in what we are calling the **JOHANSEN JUBILEE** reissues. These much-requested titles take you back to the very beginning of Iris's fabulous writing career with the first four romances she wrote, and they are **STORMY VOWS, TEMPEST AT SEA, THE RELUCTANT LARK,** and **BRONZED HAWK.** In these very first love stories published in the fall and winter of 1983, Iris began the tradition of continuing characters that has come to be commonplace in romance publishing. She is a true innovator, a great talent, and I'm sure you'll want to buy all these signed editions, if not for yourself, then for someone you care about. Could there be a better Christmas present than an introduction to the love stories of Iris Johansen? And look for great news inside each of the JOHANSEN JUBILEE editions about her captivating work coming in February, **THE WIND DANCER.** Bantam, too, has a glorious surprise that we will announce next month.

Give a big shout "hooray" now because Barbara Bowell is back! And back with a romance you've requested—**THE LAST BRADY,** LOVESWEPT
(continued)

#444. Delightful Colleen Brady gets her own romance with an irresistibly virile heartbreaker, Jack Blackledge. He's hard to handle—to put it mildly—and she's utterly inexperienced, so when he needs her to persuade his mother he's involved with a nice girl for a change, the sparks really fly. As always, Barbara Boswell gives you a sweet, charged, absolutely unforgettable love story.

A hurricane hits in the opening pages of Charlotte Hughes's **LOUISIANA LOVIN'**, LOVESWEPT #445, and its force spins Gator Landry and Michelle Thurston into a breathlessly passionate love story. They'd been apart for years, but how could Michelle forget the wild Cajun boy who'd awakened her with sizzling kisses when she was a teenager? And what was she to do with him now, when they were trapped together on Lizard Bayou during the tempest? Fire and frenzy and storm weld them together, but insecurity and pain threaten to tear them apart. A marvelous LOVESWEPT from a very gifted author!

SWEET MISCHIEF, LOVESWEPT #446, by Doris Parmett is a sheer delight. Full of fun, fast-paced, and taut with sexual tension, **SWEET MISCHIEF** tells the love story of sassy Katie Reynolds and irresistible Bill Logan. Bill is disillusioned about the institution of marriage and comes home to his childhood friend Katie with an outrageous proposition. . . . But Katie has loved him long enough and hard enough to dare anything, break any rules to get him for keeps. Ecstasy and deep emotion throw Bill for a loop . . . and Katie is swinging the lasso. **SWEET MISCHIEF** makes for grand reading, indeed. A real keeper.

Bewitching is the first word that comes to mind to

(continued)

describe Linda Cajio's LOVESWEPT #447, **NIGHTS IN WHITE SATIN**. When Jill Daneforth arrives in England determined to get revenge for the theft of her mother's legacy, she is totally unprepared for Rick Kitteridge, an aristocrat and a devil of temptation. He pursues her with fierce passion—but an underlying fear that she can never be wholly his, never share more than his wild and wonderful embraces. How this tempestuous pair reconciles their differences provides some of the most exciting reading ever!

Witty and wonderful, **SQUEEZE PLAY**, LOVESWEPT #448, from beloved Lori Copeland provides chuckles and warmth galore. As spontaneous as she is beautiful, Carly Winters has to struggle to manage her attraction to Dex Mathews, the brilliant and gorgeous ex-fiance who has returned to town to plague her in every way . . . including competing in the company softball game. They'd broken up before because of her insecurity over their differences in everything except passion. Now he's back kissing her until she melts, vowing he loves her as she is . . . and giving you unbeatable romance reading.

Sweeping you into a whirlwind of sensual romance, **LORD OF LIGHTNING**, LOVESWEPT #449, is from the extraordinary writer, Suzanne Forster. Lise Anderson takes one look at Stephen Gage and knows she has encountered the flesh-and-blood embodiment of her fantasy lover. As attracted to her as she is to him, Stephen somehow knows that Lise yearns to surrender to thrilling seduction, to abandon all restraint. And he knows, too, that he is just the man to make her dreams come true. But her fears collide with his . . . even as they show

(continued)

each other the way to heaven . . . and only a powerful love can overcome the schism between this fiercely independent schoolteacher and mysterious geologist. **LORD OF LIGHTNING**—as thrilling a romance as you'll ever hope to read.

Six great romances next month . . . four great Iris Johansen classics—LOVESWEPT hopes to make your holiday very special and very specially romantic.

With every good wish for a holiday filled with the best things in life—the love of family and friends.

Sincerely,

Carolyn Nichols

Carolyn Nichols,
Publisher,
LOVESWEPT
Bantam Books
666 Fifth Avenue
New York, NY 10103

P.S. GIVE YOURSELF A SPECIAL PRESENT: CALL OUR LOVESWEPT LINE 1-900-896-2505 TO HEAR EXCITING NEWS FROM ONE OF YOUR FAVORITE AUTHORS AND TO ENTER OUR SWEEPSTAKES TO WIN A FABULOUS TRIP FOR TWO TO PARIS!

FOREVER LOVESWEPT

SPECIAL KEEPSAKE EDITION OFFER

$12⁹⁵ VALUE

Here's your chance to receive a special hardcover Loveswept "Keepsake Edition" to keep close to your heart forever. Collect hearts (shown on next page) found in the back of Loveswepts #426-#449 (on sale from September 1990 through December 1990). Once you have collected a total of 15 hearts, fill out the coupon and selection form on the next page (no photocopies or hand drawn facsimiles will be accepted) and mail to: Loveswept Keepsake, P.O. Box 9014, Bohemia, NY 11716.

FOREVER LOVESWEPT
SPECIAL <u>KEEPSAKE</u> EDITION OFFER
SELECTION FORM

Choose from these special Loveswepts by your favorite authors. Please write a 1 next to your first choice, a 2 next to your second choice. Loveswept will honor your preference as inventory allows.

Loveswept®

_____BAD FOR EACH OTHER   Billie Green

_____NOTORIOUS   Iris Johansen

_____WILD CHILD   Suzanne Forster

_____A WHOLE NEW LIGHT   Sandra Brown

_____HOT TOUCH   Deborah Smith

_____ONCE UPON A TIME...GOLDEN
       THREADS   Kay Hooper

Attached are 15 hearts and the selection form which indicates my choices for my special hardcover Loveswept "Keepsake Edition." Please mail my book to:

NAME:_____

ADDRESS:_____

CITY/STATE:_____ZIP:_____

Offer open only to residents of the United States, Puerto Rico and Canada. Void where prohibited, taxed, or restricted. Allow 6 - 8 weeks after receipt of coupons for delivery. Offer expires January 15, 1991. You will receive your first choice as inventory allows; if that book is no longer available, you'll receive your second choice, etc.